Someone Named Eva

Joan M. Wolf

CLARION BOOKS · NEW YORK

AUTHOR'S NOTE

The characters and events in this book are fictitious. Any similarity to real persons, living or dead, is coincidental and not intended by the author. While the locations in Lidice, Czechoslovakia, Puschkau (the Nazis' name for Puszykowko), Poland, and Fürstenberg, Germany, are actual, events have been fictionalized for dramatic purposes.

Clarion Books
a Houghton Mifflin Company imprint
215 Park Avenue South, New York, NY 10003
Copyright © 2007 by Joan M. Wolf

The text was set in 13-point Aldus Roman.

www.clarionbooks.com

Printed in the U.S.A.

Library of Congress Cataloging-in-Publication Data
Wolf, Joan M., 1966–
Someone named Eva / Joan M. Wolf.
p.   cm.
Summary: Taken from her home in Lidice, Czechoslovakia, in 1942, eleven-year-old Milada is taken with other blond, blue-eyed children to a school in Poland to be trained as "proper Germans," then adopted by German families, but all the while she remembers her true name and history.
ISBN-13: 978-0-618-53579-8
ISBN-10: 0-618-53579-9
1. World War, 1939–1945—Europe—Juvenile fiction. [1. World War, 1939–1945—Europe—Fiction. 2. Boarding schools—Fiction. 3. Schools—Fiction. 4. Brainwashing—Fiction. 5. Nazis—Fiction. 6. Europe—History—1918–1945—Fiction.] I. Title.
PZ7.W819157   Som 2007
[Fic]—dc22   2006026070

MP 10 9 8 7 6 5 4

*To the children of Lidice, past and present,
and to Pat, who stepped into the darkness
to find the light*

ACKNOWLEDGMENTS

This book would never have been completed without the support and encouragement of many people, just a few of whom I would like to thank here.

Thanks to my family and friends who listened, encouraged, and helped in all steps along the way. As always, this includes Kathleen Keating and Jeanie Davis Pullen.

Thanks to the instructors in the Hamline University MFA program, who helped me find the words. A special thanks to Sheila O'Connor and Mary Rockcastle, gifted teachers and writers.

Thanks to Kate DiCamillo for her thesis insight, encouragement, and delightful sense of humor.

Thanks to Jennifer Wingertzahn, for her tireless work, amazing dedication, and incredible talent in helping to weave the pieces of the story into a complete whole.

Thanks to my agent, Ann Tobias, to whom the word "thanks" just doesn't say enough, for believing in the story and offering wise advice about all matters of writing and the writing life.

Unending thanks to Katarina Kruspanova, my guide and impromptu interpreter in Lidice, Czech Republic. And to Marie Tělupilová, director of the Lidice Memorial Museum, who gave me so many valuable resources for this book and provided a lifetime of memories during my trip to Lidice. Sadly, Marie passed away unexpectedly only a few months after my visit. I hope I have done justice in this book to her work in Lidice.

And most of all, my thanks to Miloslava Suchánek-Kalibová, Jaroslava Suchánek-Sklenička, Václav Zelenka, and Maruška (Marie) Doležalová-Supíková, four extraordinary survivors of the events in Lidice on June 10, 1942. I thank you for taking me into your hearts and sharing your stories with me. I am awed and inspired by your courage.

My sincere appreciation to Michlean L. Amir, Reference Archivist at the United States Holocaust Memorial Museum in Washington, D.C., and Dr. Teri Balkenende, adjunct professor of history at Antioch University in Seattle, Washington, who kindly read the manuscript for historical accuracy. Any mistakes, historical or otherwise, are my own.

GLOSSARY OF GERMAN WORDS

Frau	Mrs.
Fräulein	Miss
Herr	Mr.
Ja	yes
Kinder	children
Liebling	darling
Mutter	mother
Nein	no
Vater	father

one

In the spring of 1942, when the soldiers came to our town, my best friend, Terezie, and I had spent every day together, as usual. It had been warm that May, the kind of warmth that comes only in the late spring, before it gets too hot or sticky humid. Our birthdays were just a month apart, and we would both be turning eleven. We had spent many nights together planning our parties and looking at the stars.

I could gaze at the stars forever, searching for their hidden pictures and watching them glitter like crystals. Papa said that even when I was a baby, I would reach up with both fists and try to grab them from the sky. Terezie didn't like stars as much as I did, but being my best friend, she usually joined me when I went outside to look at them.

One night, a week before my birthday, we were

outside lying next to each other when there was a streak in the sky.

"Ooh, Milada, look!" Terezie leaned on one elbow and jabbed me excitedly. "A shooting star." A shooting star could only mean that something wonderful and special would happen soon.

"Make a wish, Terezie," I said, closing my eyes and thinking about what I should use my own wish for. I immediately thought of my birthday.

"I know why there's a shooting star. I know what's going to happen," Terezie said, as if she knew what I had been thinking. She had a way of doing that—of always seeming to know my thoughts even if I didn't speak them out loud.

I looked over and saw that she had a grin on her face. "Is it about my birthday?"

Terezie's smile widened and she looked away with a giggle, hugging her knees to her chest.

"You know, don't you!" I grabbed her by the shoulder. "Terezie, you know what my birthday present is. Is it a real present? Oh, please, you must tell me!"

"I am sworn to secrecy." Her giggle became a big, hearty laugh, one that was loud and musical at the same time. That laugh was one of my favorite things about her.

I had known there probably wouldn't be a present for my birthday that May, even though I hoped differently. My babichka, my grandmother, might knit a scarf or mittens from yarn that she had saved, but since the Nazis had come to Czechoslovakia three years ago, everything had been scarce. I knew better than to hope for a present that cost money.

"Stop teasing, Terezie. Mama said there wasn't even enough sugar for a cake. How could there be a present?"

"You'll just have to wait until your birthday party to find out." She made a motion as if she were zipping her lips together, and refused to say anything more.

Ever since I could remember, Terezie's family and mine had come together each May to celebrate my birthday and then again each June to celebrate Terezie's. Even with the war and rationings, this year was to be no different. And so on a beautiful Sunday afternoon in the middle of May, everyone from both families gathered in our backyard for my party. I had even been allowed to invite Zelenka and Hana, two friends from school. But Mama had also made me invite Ruzha. Like Zelenka and Hana, she was in my class, but I did not consider her a friend. She was cold and unfriendly, and she could be so mean that even the boys were afraid of her.

"Oh, Mama, no! Please?" I had begged when Mama had insisted I invite her.

"If you want to invite others, you must include Ruzha. Things have been hard on her since her mother died."

"She'll ruin my party!" I had complained. But

Mama had turned away, and I had known there would be no further discussion.

Now, as we all sat together, chatting and enjoying the beautiful day, Ruzha stood off to the side by herself. She wore a dress that she had nearly outgrown, and strands of her blond hair had come out of her barrette, falling into her eyes. She looked pained, as if she were counting the minutes until she would be dismissed. I sometimes felt that way during lessons, but never at a party. Ruzha seemed to like school, and she was a good student. But she was never the teachers' pet. The teachers, too, seemed to tire of the way she always found fault—with others and with them.

"Happy birthday, Milada!" Mama said as Papa placed a large wrapped package in my lap.

"Oh, Papa, a present!" I looked at Terezie, and she winked. Babichka, stood nearby holding my one-year-old sister, Anechka, who gurgled and stuck her fingers in her mouth.

Terezie and her two older brothers crowded close as I began to rip open the package. Suddenly, a hand appeared on top of mine.

"Jaro!" I yelled. My fifteen-year-old brother, Jaroslav, was forever pestering me. "Stop it!"

But when I looked up at him, there was a softness in his eyes. "Guess what's inside, Milada," he said. "You have to guess before you open it. That makes for good luck." For a moment it was as if I was a little girl again, when he would push me on the swing instead of constantly tormenting me, and I smiled.

Following his directions, I closed my eyes. "I think it's a doll," I teased. "Like the one I used to sleep with every night." That doll, affectionately named Mrs. Doll, still sat, ragged and torn, on a shelf in my room. Jaro constantly threatened to throw her in the trash when I wasn't looking.

Jaro let out a deep laugh. Hana and Zelenka laughed too, and I even saw a smile flicker across Ruzha's face as she watched from a distance.

Then I tore the rest of the paper from the gift, lifted the lid of the box, and sat staring at what lay inside, my mouth open in awe.

"Do you like it, Milada?" Papa asked.

"Oh, Papa." I could barely speak.

Inside the box was a telescope. The small dent on one side told me it was a used telescope, but it was the most beautiful thing I had ever seen.

"I know you like the stars. Now that you are eleven, I felt you were old enough for the responsibility of your own telescope."

"Oh, Papa!" I repeated. I put the box aside and grabbed his neck in a hug.

"I'm so glad you like it. So glad," he said, patting my shoulder.

"Here, Milada." Terezie withdrew a small wrapped package from her dress pocket. "This is for you. Happy birthday."

"Oh, Terezie. You weren't supposed to," I said.

Mama had made it very clear that there were to be only family gifts.

Terezie glanced at Mama, then at me. "Well, we're practically sisters," she said.

"Thank you," I said, unwrapping the package and unfolding what was inside. It was a hand-made movie poster. Terezie had pasted one of her movie-star photos in the middle and drawn decorations around it to make a poster like the ones that hung in the theaters. The photo was one of her favorites. It was a true gift.

"I made it myself." Terezie blushed.

"It's perfect," I said, hugging her hard.

"Dessert, everyone!" Mama announced, holding up a pan of my favorite berry dessert.

"Mama, where did you get the sugar?" I asked.

"Terezie's mother gave me some of her rations," she answered.

I looked at Terezie's mother, who smiled. "Thank you," I said. I looked around at all the people at the party. They had helped make it a special day. "Thank you, everyone."

The partly used candle from Anechka's first birthday had been lit and placed in the middle of the pastry, so it looked a little more like an actual birthday cake. I made a wish, blew out the candle, and watched Mama cut small pieces for everyone.

I took a bite, enjoying the mix of tangy fruit and sweetened dough. As we ate, the adults gathered in a group, and, as usual, their conversation turned to the topic of Hitler.

"The dessert is delicious," Papa said to Mama. Then, turning to Terezie's mother, he added, "It was so generous of you to give us your sugar rations."

"It's the least I could do," she said. "We all have to do what we can while Hitler and his Nazis are here."

"Hitler!" Babichka said sharply, then spit on the ground as she always did after speaking his name. "He is evil!"

"Mother," Papa said, touching her shoulder. "Things will improve. Don't upset yourself."

"Let's go by the tree and eat," I said to my guests. I hated seeing Babichka so upset, and I didn't want to hear about the war or spoil the good feelings of the day.

We settled on the ground under the huge tree in our yard. Even Ruzha joined us. I passed Terezie's movie poster around so everyone could get a closer look.

"I would like to be a movie actress someday," Hana said, sighing.

"You're not pretty enough," Ruzha said with her usual cutting tone.

"That's not nice," said Zelenka.

"Well, it's true," Ruzha continued. "And you have to be able to read and memorize lines to be a movie actress."

Hana's face reddened with embarrassment. Everyone knew she had struggled for a long time with learning to read.

Zelenka tried to help Hana by changing the subject. "I like the flowers in your hair, Milada."

Ruzha rolled her eyes but said nothing more.

"Thank you." I touched the small wildflowers woven into my braid. "Mama and Babichka put them in."

Terezie nodded in agreement, but I saw a look of longing in her eyes. She had always been envious of my straight blond hair. Hers was deep brown and wildly curly and unruly. Of the two of us, she was the one to worry about her hair and her looks and when she would be old enough to wear make-up. I had never cared much for dressing up or styling my hair, and I had complained loudly when Mama and Babichka had insisted on putting it in a fancy braid for the party.

Our conversation was interrupted by Mama. "Ruzha, your brother is here for you."

I looked up to see Ruzha's brother, Karel, at the edge of our yard. He looked uncomfortable, standing with his hands shoved into his pockets and shuffling from foot to foot.

"You don't need to leave right away, do you?" Mama asked as she handed him a slice of dessert.

"Thank you," he mumbled. He ate quickly, not speaking to Jaro or Terezie's brothers or even to Ruzha. Ruzha seemed even more uncomfortable with Karel there, and she too said nothing as we all sat quietly finishing our dessert.

"Ruzha. Come," Karel said gruffly when he was done eating.

Ruzha got up, and without even saying good-bye, they both left. Although I would never have said anything out loud, I was secretly glad she wasn't staying for the rest of the party. She had already been mean to Hana. I didn't want her ruining anything else.

After dessert, everyone, adults and children, divided into two teams to play our annual game of tug-of-war. This, I knew, would be followed by a game of my choice, since it was my birthday.

"Tag," I said, when it was time to pick a new game. "I choose tag!"

"Well, of course. What other game would it be?" Terezie teased. I was the fastest runner in my class, and I loved any game that involved speed.

We played many rounds of tag until the adults tired and went inside the house. Zelenka, Hana, Terezie, and I kept running around the yard, laughing and giggling as Jaro and Terezie's brothers chased us. Finally, even we grew tired and Mama declared the party over. Zelenka and Hana left first, followed by Terezie and her family. I helped Mama carry the plates and silverware into the kitchen, but she told me I didn't have to wash them since it was my birthday.

When it began to grow dark, Babichka and I sat together on the front steps. I had pulled my hair out of its braid, and it hung loose and long against my shoulders. Babichka sat on the step above me, gently brushing my hair as she did sometimes. I loved the feel of her hands and the soothing motion of the brush.

Stars had begun to appear, one by one, in the sky. I looked up, and Babichka followed my gaze. "Tonight you and your papa should try your new birthday gift and get a closer look at those stars."

"Yes," I answered. I could tell it was going to be a clear night, a good night for stargazing, with or without a telescope. My grandmother was the one who had taught me about stars and constellations, and the stories behind them. She was an expert on stars and known throughout our village as a gifted storyteller. We had spent many nights on the porch looking up at the sky together. I hoped to be just like her someday. I loved that we already shared the same name: I had been named Milada after Babichka, who had been named after her mother.

"Look, Babichka. It's Ursa Minor," I said, raising my arm and tracing the stars that formed the shape of a small water dipper.

"Yes, Milada." She nodded, looking where I pointed. "And the star, at the very end, do you remember what it's called?"

With my finger I followed the fainter stars until I reached the brightest one at the end. "Of course. It's Polaris," I said. Babichka and I had talked many times about this star.

"Yes." Babichka nodded again. "The North Star—the one star that is always in the true northern part of the sky."

Babichka had taught me that this star was also

special because it was always visible in the sky, no matter what the season. At first I hadn't believed her. I knew that constellations moved in the sky season by season and that some even disappeared temporarily. But Babichka had shown me, patiently pointing out the North Star each season for a whole year, and I had realized she was right.

"Sailors used this star to help them find their way across the sea and to help them find their way back home from long voyages," Babichka said.

I nodded, thinking of some of the stories she had told me about sailors and the stars. "Remember, Milada," she said, putting her brush down and turning my face up to look at hers. "No matter where you are, if you can see the North Star, you can find your way. Even if you're lost. It will always be there to help you find your way home."

"Yes, Babichka," I said, nodding, "I know."

She looked at me a few seconds longer, then took the brush up again and began pulling it through my hair, humming softly. I nestled in closer to her, thinking about the North Star and constellations, and we sat for a long while without talking as the light faded around us.

✳

Once it was dark, Papa and I left to try my new telescope. The sky stayed clear as we reached the hill where we usually looked at stars. I shook with excitement as Papa showed me how to adjust the dials. I had wanted a telescope since I had turned five, and now I had one.

First I looked carefully at the night sky with my own eyes. Then I looked through the lens, amazed to see the way the stars and planets changed when seen through the telescope.

"Do you want to look?" I asked Papa, who was sitting on the ground next to me.

"No, no. You go ahead. I'm happy just to sit. I have a long day in the fields tomorrow."

Papa had been a farmer his whole life, and he worked hard. He was proud of what he did and proud that his father and his grandfather had been farmers too. Often he told me that a person must be proud of the things he chooses to do.

I scanned the sky for the North Star, thinking about what Babichka had told me. Papa and I sat in silence for a while; then I asked the question I had been wanting to ask for several hours.

"Papa," I began.

"Yes?" he said, turning toward me.

"When will Hitler's Nazis leave?" I had been unable to stop thinking about this since hearing the adults talk at my party.

"Oh, Milada. This is nothing for you to worry about. Especially on your birthday."

"But they've been here for three years, and Terezie's mama said once that she doesn't think President Beneš is coming back."

I was eight when the Nazis came. A week after their arrival we had visited Mama's cousin in Prague, and I had seen the victory parade the Nazis held for Hitler. The soldiers had marched by fiercely, wearing tall black boots and black swastikas on their uniforms. We had been required to attend, and everyone had been forced to raise their right arm and say, "Heil Hitler!"

Later, a law had been passed that all Jewish people would have to wear a six-pointed yellow star on their clothes. I had been glad that no one I knew was Jewish and that I would not have to be marked this way. But remembering that parade still made me shiver.

"Everything is going to work out," Papa reassured me. "We just need to stay together as a family and a town, and this will pass. It will." Papa ruffled my hair. "I promise."

I nodded and looked back up at the sky, comforted by my father's words. I knew he wouldn't say something that he didn't believe to be true. Things would work out. He had promised.

two

June 1942: Lidice, Czechoslovakia

A few weeks after my birthday, Terezie and I got permission to stay up late, look at stars, and plan her upcoming party.

The night was warm and clear, and it seemed that every star in the universe could be seen. I showed Terezie how to use the telescope, and after looking through it for a while, we lay down on the grass to talk.

"I want dessert too, of course," Terezie said when we began to talk about the food for her party. "But I'd really like a cake—a cake with frosting. I don't know if that will be possible with so little sugar, but . . ." She stopped talking when Jaroslav suddenly appeared.

"Don't let me interrupt your dreams of sugar and cakes," he said with a smile. "I just came outside to enjoy the night air."

"Go away, Jaro. We're talking about Terezie's

birthday." Despite how nice he had been to me at my party, he could still be a pest.

"No, Milada, let him stay." Even though I couldn't see in the dark, I knew Terezie was blushing. It was no secret she had a crush on Jaroslav.

He sat on the grass quietly as we finished planning. By then it was late, so Terezie and I said goodbye. After she left, I went to bed and fell asleep, thinking about stars and birthday parties.

✳

A few hours later I was awakened by a loud, angry pounding on our front door that sent a sickening feeling down into my stomach. Something was very wrong.

Suddenly, the door banged open and the pounding was replaced by the sounds of heavy boots, barking dogs, and fierce shouting in German. Throwing my covers aside, I jumped out of bed and raced downstairs to find our living room filled with Nazi soldiers.

"Papa!" I cried. He held out a hand to stop me from coming any farther.

I felt my whole body shaking. *Nazis.* Up close they were even more frightening than when I had seen them in Prague.

And now they were in our living room.

Jaro stood quietly next to Babichka, with an arm around her shoulders. In the other room I could hear Mama taking Anechka out of her crib.

I looked from Jaro to the Nazis. The soldiers seemed almost as young as my brother, and a few of them swayed on wobbly legs. The reek of stale whiskey hung in the air.

The Nazi nearest me barked a command in German, pointing upstairs with his gun.

"Go upstairs to your room, Milada," Mama said as she entered the room with Anechka in her arms. "They are saying we must leave the house. Get dressed and take some of your things. Pack enough for three days." I couldn't understand the soldier's words, just the fear he was causing, but Mama understood German.

I turned to go upstairs, trying to get my legs to move, and suddenly the soldiers and dogs were gone. They had left the front door open, and silence stood in their place.

In school Terezie and I had once read a poem about "loud silence," and we had laughed at what the author had written. How could silence be loud? But that night, right after the Nazis left, a loud silence was what stayed behind in our house, as if it were a real thing, just as in the poem. Everything was completely quiet, but the terrifying presence of the soldiers lingered behind.

Jaro was the first to speak. "Why are they here?" He looked from Mama to Papa, then back to Papa again. "What's going on?"

"We are being arrested and taken for interrogation." Papa's voice was quiet.

"What? Why? I don't—" Jaro began, but Papa interrupted.

"I don't know, Jaro. Just follow their orders and it will get sorted out. Now pack. Go."

I dressed quickly, still not believing that Nazis had actually been in our living room and that I was packing to leave my home.

I put some clothes into a bag and tucked Mrs. Doll under one arm, even though I knew I was too old for her. Then I gently lifted my telescope down from the shelf. It would come with me wherever I went.

Downstairs, Anechka rested quietly in Mama's arms. Papa was holding a suitcase in one hand and Mama's hand in the other. Jaro stood with his traveling bag too, and a stubborn look on his face. Babichka carried nothing other than the small framed wedding picture of herself and Grandfather, who had been dead many years, and her crystal rosary beads.

I stared at her, wondering where her bag was. Why didn't she have her silver candlesticks or her crucifix? Where was her hand-stitched shawl?

She pulled me to her and grasped my hand in hers. Gently, she pressed her garnet pin into my palm. It had always been my favorite. It was shaped like a star, with tiny red stones around it that twinkled up at me in the light. I shook my head and tried to give it back.

"No, Milada." She took it out of my hand and pinned it on the inside of my blouse, her hands trembling slightly. "You must keep this and remember," she whispered, bending close to my ear. "Remember who you are, Milada. Remember where you are from. Always."

I opened my mouth to protest further.

"Shh, little one. Don't say anything. Shh." She put a finger to my lips and ran a hand through my hair.

"All right," Papa said, turning off the living-room light and turning on the porch light. "All right," he repeated, and together the six of us left our house.

Two Nazis waited in the yard with dogs. The porch light spilled across their faces, changing their features so it looked as if they were wearing masks.

One guard used his gun to direct Babichka and me to the right side of the house. The other guard grabbed Papa roughly and pulled him from Mama. I watched as Mama's and Papa's intertwined hands stretched and stretched, until at last they had to let go and Papa, his eyes filled with tears, was pulled away from Mama.

"I love you, Antonín!" Mama cried.

"I love you, Jana!" Papa's voice cracked.

The other Nazi grabbed Jaro by the arm and shoved him behind Papa, away from where Mama, Babichka, and I were standing. Jaro looked at us, blowing Mama and Babichka a kiss and winking at me. I felt myself being pushed farther and farther away from Papa and Jaro. I opened my mouth to say something, but no words came out. I could only watch them being led away, until Mama turned me in the direction the Nazis' guns pointed.

I was shaking all over and looked up, noticing the stars tucked into the folds of night. They twinkled but looked dull and listless to me and offered no comfort.

Other women and children, our neighbors, began to join us. They, too, were led by Nazis, and I realized it wasn't just my family that was being arrested. The night air filled with the sound of our feet crunching on the gravel path as every house in Lidice was emptied. Mama kissed Anechka lightly on her forehead, and I shifted the telescope in my arm, beginning to feel its weight.

"Milada!" I turned to see Terezie and her mother running to catch up to us.

"Terezie!" I cried, grabbing her in a hug. Mama gave Terezie's mother a brief kiss on the cheek, tears wetting both their faces.

"Do you know what is happening?" Terezie asked. Her eyes were puffy, and she looked scared as she slipped her hand into mine. Like us, they had no men with them. It was just Terezie and her mother.

"Papa said we're being arrested," I whispered.

"All of us? Why?" Terezie whispered back.

"I don't know," I answered.

We were stopped at the entrance to our school, where the soldiers' German commands mixed with the sounds of children sniffling and women whispering. Prodding us with their guns, the soldiers led us into the gymnasium and directed us to stand along a wall in a long single-file line. I stood close to Mama and Babichka, while Terezie sandwiched between me and her own mama.

Casually, the soldiers began grabbing our bags and suitcases, all the things we had been told to pack. A mix of fear and anger ran through me. Why had we packed just to have everything taken away from us?

As the soldiers approached Babichka, she stared straight ahead. She didn't move or show any emotion when the black-gloved hands took her wedding picture from her. It flew soundlessly, end over end, toward one of the growing piles of possessions, finally landing with a loud, splintering crash as the glass shattered.

My doll was torn from me and thrown through the air toward the same pile. But when the Nazis reached for my telescope, I felt tears come to my eyes. I shook my head, pulling away from the Nazi soldier whose hand was reaching for my precious birthday gift.

"Milada!" Mama whispered. "Obey."

I looked at her but didn't move. How could I watch my new telescope get tossed onto one of the piles like a useless rag? I looked up at the guard, trying one last time to use my eyes to plead with him. But with a rough yank he pulled the telescope free from my hand.

Instead of throwing it on the pile, though, he handed it to another Nazi, who was walking up and down the aisle, clicking his heels with importance. That guard took it and quickly disappeared into the gym locker room. I breathed a small sigh of relief. At least it hadn't been broken.

The guard barked another order in an angry, rushed tone. Quickly we were led back outside, where large trucks waited with their engines growling loudly. Each was covered with thick fabric that billowed up like a tent. Even in the dark I could see the black swastikas boldly glaring down at us.

Everyone huddled close together as we were led up the ramps like animals into the waiting trucks. Inside, guards motioned for us to sit on the small benches lining either side of the truck bed. I sat down, suddenly tired. My arm throbbed from having held my telescope, and I could no longer keep the tears back.

"Where are we going?" I whispered to Mama as the truck lurched away from our school.

"I don't know." She brushed a tear away from my face and swept my bangs out of my eyes. Anechka was almost asleep on her shoulder.

"Where are Papa and Jaroslav?" I asked. Babichka took my hand in hers and squeezed.

"Hush now, Milada," Mama said. "Just close your eyes and try to sleep." She pulled my head gently against her shoulder.

Babichka was praying softly next to me, using her free hand to finger the rosary that she had managed to keep by hiding it in her dress sleeve. Terezie and her mother sat together farther down the bench. I closed my eyes, feeling the bumpy gravel of the road, and tried not to breathe in the rancid smell of engine exhaust.

✻

I jerked when the truck lurched to a stop a few minutes later. Whispers ran up and down the benches, passing along the message that we were in Kladno, a town close to Lidice.

Nazi soldiers appeared and placed ramps at the backs of the trucks. Then we were herded into another school. This one was bigger than our school in Lidice, and we found ourselves in an even larger gymnasium.

There was hay spread across the floor, filling the air with a soft, sweet scent. Using their guns, the soldiers directed us to a place on the hay, and Mama spread out Anechka's blanket for us to sit on. My sister awoke, and her wail mixed with our hushed voices as we settled down on the floor.

Suddenly, I felt immensely tired. It was as if sleep was the only important thing. Despite the fear, the worry, and the itchiness of the hay, I fell asleep as soon as I put my head down.

✻

Rays of sun poking through the gymnasium windows woke me with a start. My body felt stiff and sore, and at first I couldn't remember where I was. But then the rustling of children awakening and the sound of women whispering brought back the events of the night before in a sickening rush.

I sat up, looking around the gym. Terezie and her mother were next to us, and my friend Hana was with her mother and sister not far away. Nearby sat her grandmother and aunt. Our widowed neighbor Mrs. Kucera was on the other side of Terezie. Across the gym I saw my teacher from last year, and near her was Zelenka with her three sisters and their mother, sitting against one of the walls. Ruzha sat with her aunt on a blanket near Zelenka, looking pale and tired.

"They can't arrest all of us," Mrs. Hanak said to her neighbor. "For what crime?" she asked to no one in particular.

Terezie's mama pleaded with a guard as he patrolled near our space, his gun held ready. "Please, sir, what has happened to my husband? When will I be able to see him again?"

He responded in clipped German without looking at her, his eyes continuing to sweep the gym. I turned to see if Mama had heard. A thin smile crossed her face, and she translated for me.

"All the men are being held at a work camp. We will go soon to join them."

Soon. That was what the guard had said. Soon I could see Papa and Jaroslav, and we would all be together again.

"None of us are Jews," Mrs. Janecek whispered loudly, trying to get one of us to talk to her. Her three children, all boys older than Jaro, had been left behind with her husband. She was alone. "Do they know this?" Her voice rose in pitch, and her eyes darted from side to side. "We are not Jews. Why are they taking us away?"

"Hush, Helena, hush." One of her neighbors patted her hand. "Hush. It will be fine. Don't start trouble. Please, please. It will be fine."

The hours passed slowly. I tried to hurry them by counting things; how many windows were at the top of the gym; how many basketballs sat on shelves along one wall; how many doors led outside; how many Nazi soldiers patrolled the rows of women and children.

Almost fifty soldiers walked among us, different ones from the night before. These men didn't look like small boys playing soldier. They were older, and they carried their guns differently. Their expressions were fixed more firmly on their faces, their eyes more focused and alert.

The sounds of women and children whispering and babies fussing echoed around us. If I closed my eyes, I could almost pretend we were at a church picnic or a school festival, rather than being held prisoner in a gym. But then I would hear someone crying or catch the scent of hay and open my eyes again to what was really happening.

Babichka continued to pray, using her crystal rosary beads. Her dress hung wrinkled on her small frame, and pieces of gray hair had begun to escape her bun. Anechka seemed unaware of the fearful things happening around her. She played patty-cake with Mama, who kept smiling and telling me everything would be fine. I smiled back, but I could see the tightness in her mouth, the worry in her eyes.

Terezie's mother joined Mama on the blanket, and they whispered back and forth to each other, their eyes avoiding both Terezie's and mine. I sat next to Terezie on her blanket, and we talked about what we were going to do when we were allowed to go back home.

"I'm going to change clothes," Terezie whispered, "and then go for a long bicycle ride."

"That sounds nice," I said. I liked the thought of riding free through the streets of Lidice on a bicycle instead of sitting in a gym on a blanket. "I think I'll do the same."

"I'll come get you and we can go together," Terezie said, nudging me with her elbow as I smiled at her.

"Yes. Then we'll make some more plans for your party. We haven't decided on dessert yet."

"I want a cake, a chocolate cake," Terezie said.

"That would be nice. We'll find the sugar somehow," I said, and Terezie nodded, smiling back at me.

✷

No one ventured far from their blanket or assigned spot. Children stayed close to their mamas, and everyone sat waiting. We were frozen in that gym like some sort of photograph, unable to do anything except wait until we could return to our homes and see our fathers and brothers again.

I wanted to hug Papa hard, harder than I ever had. I wanted to feel the roughness of his beard and hear his deep voice and gravelly laugh. I wanted him to know about my telescope. I wanted to hear him say that he was proud I had tried to keep it from the Nazis, and that somehow we would get a new one so I could continue to look at the stars.

I wanted to see Jaro, too. To give him a hug and let him tease me about the doll I had brought with me. And to see Terezie blush in front of him again.

Instead, all of us sat and waited. The minutes ticked away into hours, the hours turning into another day. The air was hot and sticky by then, and the hay had become itchy and thin. My stomach had grown impatient with hunger. We had been given nothing to eat but cold coffee and pieces of dry bread, and there had been hardly enough for everyone. I watched with envy as Anechka sucked her bottle, wishing Mama had brought food for me, too.

Women had begun to move about more freely, stopping to talk with neighbors or sitting in small huddled groups to pray quietly. But all the while, we were being watched carefully by the Nazis with their guns.

Toward the end of our second afternoon of waiting, two men with clipboards and white coats came down a small set of stairs at the back of the gym. The guards ignored the men as they walked through the rows of women and children. But we watched warily as they moved from blanket to blanket, looking at each child and muttering in German while writing notes on their clipboards. Occasionally, one of the men would call over a guard, who would use his gun to direct a child to stand and walk up the same set of stairs at the back of the gym.

When one of the men came to Terezie, he looked at her briefly, wrote something on his clipboard, and quickly moved on. He came to my blanket next and stopped, taking a strand of my hair in his hand. Gently he rubbed it between two fingers, murmuring softly to himself.

"Ja." He nodded with a quick smile and scribbled something on his clipboard. Then he motioned to a guard, who pulled me up from the blanket. I was to follow the other children up the stairs.

"Mama?" I asked, looking down at her and Anechka sitting on the blanket. Even though it was very warm in the gym, I suddenly felt cold. Anechka reached up for me, her little fingers opening and closing.

"Go with them, Milada. You must obey." Babichka was the one who spoke, pointing to the place where her pin lay under my shirt. I had forgotten about the pin, and I looked into her face, trying to gather courage.

"Go, Milada. Do as they say. I love you," Mama said, squeezing my hand in hers.

Taking a deep breath, I joined the line of children

walking to the back of the gym. Terezie's eyes met mine briefly as I walked by her blanket.

A Nazi led us up the stairs and into a small room at the end of a hall. Two boys younger than me and a girl closer to Jaro's age followed me, and we joined about a dozen other Lidice children already standing in what looked like a science classroom. I stopped in the doorway, amazed by what I saw.

It wasn't who was there that surprised me. I recognized most everyone from school, although there was only one other person from my class: Ruzha. She stood on the other side of the room. Boys and girls from the lower grades through year six had been gathered and were standing at the front of the room by the blackboard.

But all of us had one thing in common, something I would not have noticed had we not been put together in one room. Each of us had blond hair and light-colored eyes.

My thoughts were interrupted by the snap of a Nazi command. There was a pause; then the guard repeated his command, sending the same sickening feeling into my stomach as when I hadn't been able to understand the Nazis in our living room. I looked around, seeing a puzzled expression in the eyes of others.

None of us knew what the guard wanted us to do as we stood shaking by the blackboard, underneath a model of the solar system. Books were scattered around the shelves, and animal cages stood empty in the corner, adding to the feeling of desolation in the room.

Two men with white coats and stethoscopes stood on the opposite side of the room. They held clipboards and were laughing and talking in German, ignoring what was happening at the front of the room. A woman in a uniform stood on one side of the blackboard, staring blankly into the open room.

The two men in white coats from the gym had also arrived, and were standing with the other men, talking quietly. I had not seen them wearing stethoscopes in the gym. Perhaps they were doctors.

They all seemed very bored, as if what they were doing was a normal part of every day. One doctor smoked a cigarette casually. Another yawned, looked over at us, then turned back and continued laughing with the others. None of them even seemed to care that we had been taken from our homes and couldn't understand their language or intentions.

"What do they want?" I whispered to a year-six girl standing next to me.

"I don't know," she whispered back, her eyes wide.

"Undress. Now!" the female Nazi finally screamed in Czech. She stepped over to grab each of us by the arm, pulling us out of our huddled group and into a crooked single-file line in front of the blackboard. I felt my face grow warm.

"Undress!" the woman repeated, reaching over and ripping down one boy's pants. Immediately, the rest of us began to undress, afraid of what would happen if we didn't.

I threw off my blouse and skirt, trying to keep my eyes on a poster hanging on the opposite wall and ignore the shame I felt as I stripped to my underwear. Not even Jaro had seen me undressed before. I dropped my clothes in a pile at my feet and stood waiting.

After everyone was undressed, the woman who had given the order grabbed each of us again and divided us up into four lines. The four men with the stethoscopes stopped talking, and each took a position at the head of a line. The woman pointed to the lines, indicating that we were to travel from one to the next.

The doctor in the first line asked me my name.

"Milada Kralicek," I answered quietly. He nodded, running his finger down his clipboard and making a note with his pen. Then he checked my mouth, nose, and eyes, using the same kind of instruments my own doctor used. He listened to my heart with his stethoscope and made me cough and do jumping jacks. He ran his finger up and down my back, then bent over his clipboard and scribbled some more with his pen. I relaxed a little as he continued. This was just a doctor's exam after all.

But in the second line the exam changed. Even though the doctor had a stethoscope and wore a white coat, he seemed interested only in my hair. Guiding me toward the wall, he placed me in front of posters, each showing a different hair color. Next he picked up a long narrow board that had small bundles of blond hair attached to it. Carefully, he took each of my braids and laid it flat against the different hair bundles, then wrote notes on his clipboard. I had a sudden urge to take the pair of scissors on the table near him and cut off all of my hair. I didn't like the way the doctor touched it.

In the next line the doctor stood near a table that had strange metal instruments on it. One of them reminded me of the silver salad tongs Mama used on special occasions, but unlike Mama's, these came to a very small point at each end. The man carefully placed each of the points on either side of my nose, pressed slightly, then wrote something down on his clipboard. He seemed to be measuring my nose. How was the size of my nose part of a doctor's exam?

Next, he took another instrument that looked like a pair of knitting needles connected by a piece of metal. He put one pole on either side of my forehead.

"Perfect!" he said in Czech, and scribbled more notes. The female Nazi stood watching that line. She smiled at the man and then at me. I turned my eyes downward, not sure what I had done to please these people, but knowing I didn't like it.

In the last line the doctor stood in front of two posters covered with pictures of eyes. He was short, bald, and fat, and he smiled at me when it was my turn. I looked away, avoiding his gaze. In his hand he held something that looked like a ruler, but it had small glass eyes in different colors glued to it. Taking my chin in one hand, he placed the ruler near my cheek with his other hand and moved it beneath my eyes until he seemed to find a matching color. Making clicking noises with his tongue, he smiled again, this time to himself, and wrote some notes on his clipboard. With a wave he dismissed me, and the female Nazi directed me back to my clothes.

I dressed quickly and was led downstairs and back into the gym. Everything looked the same. The Nazis still patrolled. The women and the other children still sat on their blankets, waiting. I could barely keep from running back to the blanket where Mama and Babichka sat playing with Anechka.

"Milada!" Terezie grabbed me in a hug, and Anechka reached out a small hand to touch my face as I collapsed on our blanket. My whole body shook uncontrollably. Terezie was called back to her blanket by her mama, and Babichka put her arm around me, letting me rest my head against her shoulder. Mama stroked my hair.

"Mama," I said.

"Yes, Milada?"

"There were doctors there. They listened to my heart and looked in my mouth, but then they looked at my hair and my eyes and measured my nose. Did they do that here, too?"

"No, Milada," she answered.

I looked closely at her. "I didn't like the way they

touched my hair, Mama. All the children there had blond hair."

A look passed between Mama and Babichka. "Perhaps they were examining the children to make sure you are healthy for a work camp," Babichka said.

"But . . ." It was difficult to ask the question I needed to. "We're not going back home, are we?" I felt a lump in my throat.

"I don't know, Milada. I don't know," Babichka answered, looking away from me and my question.

✳

We stayed in the gym the rest of that day and night and into a third day. Tension grew high. The hay that had at first smelled sweet and inviting was now pungent, having absorbed the sour smell of our worry and fear. Everyone was growing angry and impatient.

"I want to see my husband!" Mrs. Janecek yelled at her neighbor. "I want to see my sons. Waiting, waiting. I am tired of this waiting!"

I was tired of counting things, tired of talking to friends, tired of pretending we would still have Terezie's birthday party. Every part of me was tired. I had been in the same clothes for three days with hardly anything to eat. Mama had snapped at me because I had not come quickly enough when she called me away from Terezie. And even Anechka was getting fussy. I didn't think I could stand another day of waiting in the gym.

Finally, as the sun was crawling down the windows, the Nazis started shouting orders.

Everyone stood, gathering the few things they had. Mama pulled me up, taking Anechka's blanket. "We are going now, Milada."

I felt a rush of relief. I just wanted to leave, to be able to move around, to see Papa and Jaro, maybe even to sleep in my own bed again. I stood eagerly, feeling almost cheerful suddenly. I helped Mama to fold the blanket and Babichka to brush bits of hay from her dress. Perhaps we were at the end of this nightmare.

One of the guards yelled another command in German, and Mama stopped, frozen, her face tightening.

"What did he say, Mama? What did he say?" I asked, frustrated that I could never understand the Nazis' words.

"He said we are all going to the work camp to see our husbands, but the children will go separately, in a more comfortable bus." She bit her lower lip, and I felt my stomach tighten. I didn't care about riding in comfort. I would stay with Mama and Babichka and Anechka. I grabbed Mama's hand and squeezed. Around us mothers pulled children toward them, and everyone stood, waiting again, like a giant cuckoo clock that had stopped in mid chime.

Then a Nazi grabbed a little girl away from her mother.

"No! No! My baby!" her mother screamed, and

the spell was broken. Everyone began running and screaming, the cuckoo clock erupting back into chaotic motion.

Mothers grasped their children while Nazis tried to pull them away. Everything was blurry movement and roaring noise until a gunshot, loud and pure and pointed, rang out through the gym. We all dropped to the ground in immediate silence.

The Nazi who had fired the gun spoke slowly and loudly, making it clear we had no choice. Every guard had his gun drawn and ready.

Babichka squeezed me hard, touching the place on my shirt where she had pinned her garnet star, and kissed my forehead.

Then Mama pulled me to her. "I love you, Milada."

"I love you, Mama." As she grasped my hand, I felt a soldier take hold of me around the waist, pulling me away from her. "No!" I screamed. But my feet were lifted from the ground, and this time it was my hand, not Papa's, that was being stretched and stretched, until I could no longer touch Mama's.

I continued reaching for her even as the soldier carried me out the door of the gym, into the late-afternoon sun, and onto a waiting bus.

I stood at the front of the bus on wobbly knees, feeling dizzy and sick to my stomach. The bus was entirely empty except for two Nazi women, the driver, and one other girl from Lidice, who sat staring at me from a seat at the back. It was Ruzha.

I stayed where I was, unable to move. Where were all the other Lidice children? Again I wished I knew German, so I could explain that there had been a mistake. They had said in the gym that all the children would ride the bus, but there were only two of us. Where were Terezie and Zelenka and Hana? What was happening to Mama and Babichka and Anechka?

One of the Nazi women walked up the aisle toward me and led me to a seat near the front, where I fell into the comfort of crushed velvet. I was glad she had not taken me to sit near Ruzha. There had already been one mistake. Sitting with Ruzha would just be another.

The bus pulled away from the curb, and I sat staring out the window, driving away from everyone I had ever known. My whole world was changing, and I was filled with dread about the new one unfolding before me.

three

We drove for hours across the countryside of Czechoslovakia. Ruzha stayed in her seat at the back of the bus, and I stayed in mine near the front, watching the land outside pass by the windows. Thoughts of Mama and Babichka and Anechka and Jaro and Papa swirled in my mind. I knew they would come for me. I just had to wait and follow directions. I could hear Papa's voice reminding me. *Sit up straight and do as you're told, Milada.* I usually heard those words from him on important occasions: my first day of school, my first communion, when my uncles came to visit. *Do as you are told.*

His words reassured me now that if I behaved and listened, I would be taken back home and this would all be nothing more than a bad dream.

I looked out the window, watching the scenery change. I had never been farther away from my village than Prague. In Lidice everything was flat and open and wide. If you stood on the highest hill near our village, you could see for miles across the fields. But as we drove, the trees and bushes grew thicker. Mountains, blue and hazy and mysterious, appeared in front of us. They stood proudly, like sentinels guarding the countryside.

As the sun began to set, a large sign reading "Polen" appeared ahead. A long gate blocked the road, and armed Nazi soldiers patrolled in front of it. There were small buildings on either side of the road, with a guard standing in each. We had reached the border of Czechoslovakia.

The bus slowed, and a guard came out of one of the buildings. He gave directions to the soldiers, and they unlocked the gate and rolled it back from the road so we could pass. The guard smiled and waved us through. The bus driver and the female Nazi sitting near me returned his wave and we drove by, picking up speed once again.

We were in Poland.

I had looked back at Ruzha a few times, but each time, she had been pressed against the window, watching the scenery pass. The one time our eyes had met, we had both quickly looked away, neither of us really wanting to talk to the other.

One of the Nazi women offered me fresh bread and something sweet and hot to drink. My stomach cried out for the food, and I gulped it down as darkness settled in.

Eventually, the bus turned off the main road and traveled down a lonely stretch of gravel highway, passing a small sign that read "Puschkau." The road was bumpy, with many holes and ruts. In the twilight the mountains had become nothing more than hulking, formless black shapes in the distance.

Finally, we pulled into a small paved parking area and stopped. Although it was dark, lights framed a small church and a building close to the parking area. The buildings stood alone, absent of trees or plants of any kind. A thin razor-wire fence glinted in the light, surrounding the church, then disappearing behind the longer building. For the first time since leaving the gymnasium, I felt hope. Perhaps this was the work camp where I would meet up with the other children.

I turned in my seat to see Ruzha still pressed against her window. Then I heard a sound and turned back to my own window to find that a second bus had stopped next to ours.

My heart jumped as I saw girls, most of them about my age, getting off the bus. I scanned their faces, looking for Terezie or Zelenka or Hana. But I recognized no one.

One of the Nazi women spoke in German, motioning with an arm for us to follow as she got off the bus. Ruzha walked past me, looking straight ahead. I followed them out onto the black pavement of the parking area. My legs felt sore and stiff from sitting for so long.

The girls from the other bus stood there, talking quietly. I counted twelve in all, and even in the poor light I could see they all had blond hair. I looked at Ruzha, noticing, as if for the first time, that she too had light-colored hair. I played with a strand of my own hair absently. Was it a coincidence?

The girls from the other bus spoke to each other in a language I didn't understand. It was not Czech, and it didn't sound German. Perhaps they were from Poland.

Some of the girls had pale faces and puffy eyes that scanned and searched this strange place we'd been brought to. None of us made eye contact with anyone else, but when I accidentally caught a glance from one of the girls, I couldn't help but stare. Her eyes were the prettiest blue I had ever seen. I smiled briefly, and she smiled back.

Two different Nazi women appeared from the door of the building and led us all into a large entry room. The floor was brightly polished, with clean white tiles glaring up at us. The walls, too, smelled clean and fresh, giving off the faint scent of new paint. On one wall was a shadowy hint that a large cross had once hung there. I thought of Babichka with her rosary in her fingers.

One of the Nazis motioned for us to follow and led us into a long, narrow sleeping room. There were fourteen cots arranged in two rows with an aisle running down the middle of the room. Moving briskly, the guard showed us each to a cot, then exited abruptly, leaving us to stand awkwardly in our new surroundings.

Here, too, the walls smelled of fresh paint, and the tile floor gleamed spotlessly. At the foot of each cot was a trunk, and above each bed hung a small photograph of Hitler, one arm outstretched in the Nazi salute. From the wall opposite the door, he glared down fiercely in an almost-life-size picture, his eyes piercing every corner of the room. Again there were shadows on the wall on either side of the picture, revealing that another cross had once hung there.

Ruzha had been assigned to the cot on my right. The girl with the pretty blue eyes had been directed to the one on my left. We all sat wearily on our cots, not sure what to do next. My mind felt blank and empty, unable to grasp anything that had happened.

Ruzha and I sat for a long while, just looking at each other, until finally she spoke.

"I don't like you, you know, Milada."

I nodded. I didn't like her either.

She continued. "I don't know what is happening, but I shouldn't be here. There's been a mistake."

"Yes," I agreed.

"A terrible mistake."

We were interrupted as a female guard came in. She motioned for us to stand and make the same salute that Hitler was making in the pictures that hung above our cots. We were to face the huge picture of Hitler opposite the door. As I raised my arm, I shuddered at the thought of Babichka seeing me. What would she have said? Her oldest granddaughter saluting a picture of the man she thought was Satan himself, in a place that had once held a cross.

I held my arm at the proper angle, but I refused to look at Hitler. This one time I would not follow Papa's advice to do as I was told.

After a minute in this pose, we were allowed to put our arms down. Then each of us was given a long white nightgown that smelled like bleach. I'd worn the same set of clothes for so many days that the nightgown felt soft and comforting against my skin, even though it smelled strange. I ran my fingers down the front of it, tracing the soft pleats of lace.

Carefully I folded my blouse and skirt the way Mama had taught me, and placed them at the foot of the cot. Then I crawled into bed. The guard left, and the lights went out.

That's when I remembered Babichka's pin. I sat up and felt for my clothes. I reached into my blouse and found the pin, unclasped it, and repinned it carefully to the inside of my nightgown. *Babichka*, I thought, trying not to cry.

The room was filled with the soft sounds of girls crying quietly in the dark.

"Milada?" It was Ruzha. Her voice sounded small.

"Yes?" I answered.

"What do you think is happening?"

"I don't know."

There was silence from her cot. Everything in the room was dark and muddled, and I could feel all the strength draining from my body. Where were Mama, Anechka, and Babichka? Why was I not with them? All I wanted was to go to sleep and awake back in my own bed in Lidice in time for Terezie's birthday party.

Compared to the sour hay and the hardness of the gym floor, the cot felt soft and comforting. Running my fingers around the bumpy outline of Babichka's pin, I let the tears finally roll onto my pillow and closed my eyes.

✳

It was still dark the next morning when the sweet sound of music threaded its way into my sleep. I could hear the beautiful Czech national anthem calling to me from our phonograph in the living room and Anechka fussing in her crib to be picked up.

> *Where is my home? Where is my home?*
> *Where brooks rumble through the meadow,*
> *Pines murmur over the mountainside,*
> *All the orchards are in bloom.*
> *What an earthly paradise in view,*
> *This is the beautiful land,*
> *The land of Czechs, home of mine.*

But as I awoke, the sounds changed. It was not my beautiful country's song. I was not home listening to Anechka's waking cry. I was far away on a small cot, listening to Ruzha cry while the tinny sounds of a German song swelled from a phonograph I couldn't see. Groggy, I sat up and turned to Ruzha.

"Oh, Milada." She was sitting on her cot, twisting her nightgown in her hands. "Oh, Milada." This time she did not avoid my eyes and I did not avoid hers.

"It's all right, Ruzha. It's all right." I sat up, still trying to shake off sleep and very aware of how close my own tears were to falling. I tried to hold them back, afraid that if they started, they would never stop.

"I don't know what's happening," Ruzha continued.

"Neither do I." I stood as the same two female guards from the night before appeared and began moving around the room briskly, motioning for us to dress.

Everyone was awake but moving slowly. My whole body felt thick and heavy, as if I was moving through mud. The desire for more sleep kept pulling me back toward my cot.

I looked around for my clothes, but they were gone. In their place was a uniform: a short-sleeved white shirt, a short dark-blue skirt, and a black scarf with a clasp engraved with an eagle. The eagle's wings were spread wide, and it clutched a tiny swastika in its talons. Confusion swept through me. When had my clothes been taken, and why? I touched Babichka's pin, still safe beneath my nightgown. I was glad I had put it there the night before.

Carefully, I pinned the star to the inside of my uniform shirt so no trace of it would show. I realized now that it needed to stay with me always.

As they dressed, the other girls spoke to one another in the same language I had heard the night before. I sat on my cot, watching them in the daylight, unable to stop staring at the blond hair crowning every girl's head.

A very small girl sat across the aisle from me, speaking in rapid, panicked tones. Most of the other girls seemed close to my age, but this girl looked very young, maybe five or six. She was having a difficult time getting her shirt buttoned. An older girl was trying to help her.

The young girl fell onto her cot crying, and the other girl hovered above, moving from foot to foot, as if unsure of what to do. Eventually, she sat down and whispered in the young girl's ear. Finally, the little girl smiled and stood up.

The Nazi women reappeared and led us down the hall to a dining room. It had a high ceiling, and tall windows lined one side. Several small tables dotted the room, and one long formal table ran down the middle.

The guards led us to the large table and directed

each girl to a chair. No one was allowed to sit until we had all given the Nazi salute. One of the guards then seated herself at the head of the table, and a woman with a cook's apron scurried back and forth to a kitchen behind the dining room. On the table were cloth napkins and dishes made of china.

Steaming bowls of sweetened oatmeal and warm loaves of bread with butter sat on the table. The smell of the food made me aware of how terribly hungry I was. I dove into the meal, eating without stopping, until every bit in front of me was gone. There seemed to be no ration books or shortages of anything here.

The other girls around me ate just as quickly, and no one spoke. The only sound in the room was the clinking of our spoons against our dishes. As I licked the last of the sugary oats from my bowl, I thought of Terezie wanting a real cake for her birthday. Guilt formed a small lump in my throat, making it difficult to swallow.

After everyone had finished breakfast, we were led into a small auditorium across from the dining hall. On the stage stood one of the Nazi women from the night before. She was pretty, in a sharp sort of way, with a small nose and soft, ivory skin. A crisp light-blue shirt and skirt fit snugly on her body, and her light-colored hair was swept up in a fancy braid wound around her head.

"Young women of the future," she said, and it was like hearing music. For the first time since leaving my home, I could understand what a Nazi was saying, because she was speaking in my language. She spoke first in Czech and then in the language the other girls had been speaking.

"It is tragic that your families were killed in an Allied air raid," the woman continued.

The frightening scene of the Nazi soldiers in our living room flashed through my mind. I could still feel the hands of the soldier around my waist, pulling me away from Mama in the gym. Didn't this woman know what had happened, how we had arrived in this place? There had been no Allied air raid. Nazis, like her, had taken us away.

Ruzha looked briefly at me, her eyes piercing mine, but I couldn't read what was in them. The woman spoke in the other girls' language, then continued in Czech.

"You are blessed to be chosen as Aryan children, sent by God to serve Hitler and save the world from the Jewish scourge."

The words "Aryan" and "Jewish" bounced around in my mind. I knew only that Jews were supposed to wear yellow stars, and I had heard the word "Aryan" just once or twice before and didn't even know what it really meant. Why was this Nazi using the word "Aryan" to describe me?

I looked around the auditorium. Each wall had a picture of Hitler, with a red candle burning beneath it. Beside each picture were posters of girls wearing uniforms similar to the ones we had been given. In some of the posters the girls wore sashes with German words running down the front.

I thought of the day Babichka, Jaro, and I had walked to church, right after Czechoslovakia had surrendered to Hitler. A picture of Hitler had been pasted on the door of the church. Babichka's eyes widened when she saw it, then filled with a hardness I had never seen. Standing tall and straight, she marched to the door, grabbed the poster, and tore it into little pieces. Her fingers moved quickly and steadily, as if she was knitting.

"Babichka! It is illegal!" Jaro took her by the shoulder, guiding her into the church while I followed behind, watching pieces of the poster flutter in the wind.

"Here, in this center," the Nazi woman continued in Czech, opening her arms wide, "you will learn everything you need to know to be a proper German girl. Everything you require will be provided. When the time is right, you will be sent out into the world to fulfill your duties as German wives and mothers. Heil Hitler!" One of the other guards stepped to the front of the small stage and motioned with her gun for us to stand and give the Hitler salute.

Then a different Nazi woman guided us to stand in a single-file row in front of the stage, facing the empty chairs in the audience. She, too, wore a blue uniform. Her hair was pulled into a neat braid, and her eyes were sharp and bright.

Next, the pretty woman who had spoken in

Czech stepped down from the stage to stand in front of our line. She pointed to herself, saying "Fräulein Krüger." Then she pointed to us, wanting us to repeat her name, which we did. Next, she approached us one at a time and said a different name for each of us.

"Franziska!" she said loudly, as she placed her hand on Ruzha's head. "Franziska!"

"Franziska!" we all repeated.

"Eva!" Now it was my turn. "E-va!" she repeated, her hand pressing down on my head.

I shook my head, shivering at the sound of this strange new word echoing in the room. My name was not Eva. Ruzha's name was not Franziska. My name was Milada, the name of my grandmother and her mother before her.

"No," I said forcefully. "My name is Milada."

"Nein!" Fräulein Krüger yelled. She slapped my face hard, moving so close to me that our noses almost touched. "Nein!" she repeated, grabbing my chin in her fingers and pressing her nails into my skin as she lifted my face toward hers. My cheek stung, and I swallowed to keep back the tears.

"E-va." She jabbed a finger into my chest. "Franziska!" She pointed at Ruzha. "Ja?"

I nodded, as a sickening feeling settled into my stomach. No longer would I be known as Milada, fastest runner in the class, stargazer, Jaroslav's little sister. No longer would I hear the lyrical sound of my own language or feel it roll across my tongue.

I returned to my seat, only half listening as Fräulein Krüger continued assigning everyone a new name. The girl with the pretty eyes became Liesel. The small girl who had had trouble buttoning her shirt, and who still stood weeping and trembling, was renamed Heidi. The girl who had helped her, her sister, was renamed Elsa.

Only part of me was at this place. The other part of me was back in Lidice, sitting under the huge tree in our backyard, listening to the crows and the sounds of summer. I was walking barefoot in the creek that ran through the center of town, feeling the crisp, cold water numb my toes. I was off visiting Mrs. Janecek's docile cows that liked to munch clover from my hand through the fence. This was where I would stay, I decided, in my memories of my home, until Mama or Papa came to rescue me.

A hand tapped my shoulder and I looked up, startled out of my thoughts, to find a Nazi guard motioning for me to follow the other girls. We walked as a group on a tour of the center. Fräulein Krüger led us, smiling and speaking in German the entire time. Besides the auditorium and sleeping room, the building had classrooms and a gymnasium. Outside, a little past the church, Fräulein Krüger pointed to the razor-wire fence that surrounded the compound in a neat square. She was no longer smiling.

She spoke in clipped, harsh German and turned

her bright eyes on each of us, then pointed to the fence that could be seen in every direction. Although I couldn't understand her words, the message was clear. There was no escape, no running away.

We walked back in silence except for the chatter of Fräulein Krüger, who had become eerily cheerful again. Along the way I looked for other buildings, other people, and any roads or paths that might lead to my rescue—any way for Papa to come find me. But there was nothing, only open, empty space and the distant shadows of the mountains.

Our tour ended with one last message delivered by Fräulein Krüger in Czech. She swept a pointed finger across our line. "You will not speak any language but the chosen Aryan language of German. Ever. Should you disobey, you will be punished. Severely."

I stood listening to the birds in the trees, wondering how they could sing, how Fräulein Krüger could smile, and how everything else in the world could go on as if nothing was happening in this once-holy place that had been turned into something awful.

Ruzha stayed next to me as we walked, but neither of us tried to speak. Even though we were together, we were very much apart.

Later that night on my cot, as the lights were turned off and the sound of girls whispering faded, I spoke my name softly to myself: *Milada, Milada, Milada.* I pictured each of my family members, and remembered what my grandmother had said as I traced the bumpy outlines of her pin.

Remember who you are, Milada. Remember where you are from. Always.

four

Each day began before the sun was up. The strains of what I now knew was the German national anthem would swell into our small room until all fourteen of us were awake and standing by our cots. With hands outstretched in salute to the large picture of Hitler on the wall, we waited to be released by Fräulein Krüger so we could dress and prepare for the day. Freshly cleaned and pressed uniforms were waiting for us each morning, along with new ribbons for our hair. Every day I secretly pinned Babichka's star to my shirt to keep it close, before walking to breakfast with everyone else.

Breakfast was always delicious and nourishing, with real sugar and delicacies such as fresh meat and fruit. Nutrition was important, we would learn in home economics lessons. Proper nutrition helped German bodies, and therefore Germany herself, grow strong. We had plenty of food, more than I had seen in years, and plenty of new clean clothes. All our physical needs were taken care of. Fräulein Krüger and the other Nazi guards and teachers were outwardly friendly, but there was always something sharp and distant about their actions.

Breakfast was followed by lessons and drills and exercises. At first, from morning until night, we studied only the German language. After our first day no adult ever translated again. Instead, gestures and signs were used if needed. We remembered the warning that the punishment for speaking in any language other than the true Aryan language of German would be severe.

During those first few weeks at the center, we spent endless hours practicing the formation and pronunciation of German words. Our language instructor, Fräulein Schmitt, was both animated and deadly serious about her lessons. When she wasn't speaking, she pursed her lips together in a way that reminded me of a bird's beak. Her hair was always pulled back so tightly that it made my head hurt just to look at it.

"Kin-der!" she would bark, cracking our desks in time to the rhythm of the words with the ruler she carried.

"Kin-der!" we repeated, as her little bird eyes darted among us, trying to catch someone mispronouncing the word.

Franziska grasped the German language quickly

and easily, and she appeared to enjoy the lessons. The words rolled effortlessly off her tongue as her eyes shone up at Fräulein Schmitt.

She was eager to point out mistakes made by the other girls in their pronunciation of German words. When someone misspoke, her hand would quickly rise high in the air.

"Yes, Franziska," the teacher would call on her, and I would know what was to come.

"Excuse me," she would say, in her beautiful German. "I do not believe that is entirely correct." And she would go on to point out the correct formation of the words or the exact inflection of the German accent.

"Yes, yes, Franziska. You are such a good student!" The teacher would praise her immensely.

And Franziska was always right. She worked hard to master this new language and received constant praise from all the teachers. In this place she was admired and respected by adults for her complete devotion to the rules and her critical eye. Other girls began to notice this favored status. Some even started to sit next to her in an attempt to receive the same special attention.

Unlike Franziska, I had a difficult time mastering the German words and phrases. My mind was muddled, trying to place the new words next to the old ones I had grown up speaking. Nothing, new or old, seemed to fit together anymore.

One night, after a very hard day of language lessons, I burst into tears of frustration. "I hate this language. I hate German. I hate the Nazis!" I cried softly in the dark from my cot.

"Eva," Franziska said quietly from her own cot. "German is the Aryan language, the true language."

"But . . ." My words trailed off as I saw the night guard pass by the door on her rounds. I closed my eyes and pretended to sleep, deciding not to finish what I had started to say—that neither of us was Aryan or German.

✷

Heidi, the little girl who had arrived with her sister, was struggling even more than I was. One hot day in August, during language lessons, Fräulein Schmitt gave us a ten-minute break away from studies. Everyone was sweaty and tired from the long drills. The windows were open and several fans were on, but only hot air circulated. We were all feeling irritable and short-tempered.

Heidi and her sister, Elsa, were seated at their desks. Across from them sat two girls who bunked near them, Siegrid and Gerde. All four were discussing ways to keep cool. Gerde and Siegrid were arguing that fans did not help when it got too hot. Heidi and Elsa argued that they did.

"The blades of a fan don't cool the air. They just move it around," Gerde said in near-perfect German. Fräulein Schmitt, who had been listening from across the room, smiled.

"Nein. The air moves faster with a fan, and that

cools it," Elsa argued. Her German sounded almost as good as Gerde's, and she, too, got a smile from the teacher. Heidi sat at her desk wiggling with impatience and eager to join the conversation with her own thoughts. But when she spoke, she used words I could not understand. Everyone in the room stopped what they were doing and looked at her. Franziska actually stood up from her desk, gaping at Heidi with wide eyes.

Heidi had spoken in Polish.

"Heidi!" Fräulein Schmitt snapped to attention. Her eyes latched onto the small girl like a hawk that had found its prey. No one else in the room moved. Fräulein Schmitt walked purposefully to Heidi, lifted her from the chair by her arm, and, as everyone watched, lifted her skirt and pulled down her underwear. With her ruler she hit Heidi five times on bare skin, a sickening *thrack, thrack* echoing in the room with each strike. When she was done, Fräulein Schmitt pushed the small girl to the floor, then crossed her arms and watched Heidi scramble to get her clothes back on.

That night angry welts appeared on Heidi's skin where the ruler had struck. We were all kept awake by her cries and the sounds of Elsa trying to comfort her.

I grew more and more angry as I listened to Heidi's moans. Who were these people, these Nazis? Why were they trying to make me one of them, with their language and their salutes and their uniforms?

I knew Mama and Papa would come for me eventually. And when they found me, we would all watch Heidi beat Fräulein Schmitt with a ruler, and then we would go home. There would be a big party, and I would make sure to take sugar so we could have a real cake to celebrate the Nazi defeat.

✵

As we began to master the German language, our lessons changed to include German history and home economics. Fräulein Krüger made a special appearance to tell us about the League of German Girls, an organization for Nazi girls. There was another group called the Hitler Youth, for Nazi boys. We were still too young to be official members, but the League of German Girls philosophy and activities guided everything we did. It was during this lesson that I finally grew to understand the word "Aryan" and to see why everyone at the center had blond hair and light-colored eyes.

"In this room you will learn of the tragic persecution of Germany after the Great War. You will also learn of the glorious salvation our Führer has brought to Germany," Fräulein Haugen, our history instructor, began on our first afternoon of her lessons. "You will learn how you, as part of the Aryan race, are far superior to others, most especially to Jews, who are no better than the rats that live on the streets."

Aryan. That word was repeated over and over again. Fräulein Haugen explained that certain things about us, such as our blond hair and light-colored eyes, made us part of the Aryan race, a group of people Hitler deemed superior to all other races.

"You will learn how *you*, chosen young Aryan girls, are the German salvation." She walked briskly between our rows of desks, the short heels of her black shoes clicking and punctuating each of her words.

"You are all so very important," she continued, as she reached down and softly touched Franziska's hair. "When you go out into the German world, you will help Hitler usher Germany into greatness once again." Franziska's eyes followed Fräulein Haugen, her head nodding in agreement.

I fingered my own hair, looking at the light-blond strands. "Straw" was what Jaro would call my hair when he was teasing. "Sun-kissed" was how Papa always described it. Either way, it was the color of my hair that had brought me to this place.

One day we came to class to find a movie projector sitting at the front of the room. I had seen very few picture shows in my life, and despite where I was and what I was learning, I was excited to see another.

"This film," Fräulein Haugen said, as she wound the film onto the reel, "will help you better understand your Aryan heritage, and the scourge of the Jews."

My stomach sank with disappointment. I didn't understand why Hitler hated the Jewish people so much. There were no Jews in Lidice, and I knew nothing of their beliefs or traditions. How could one group of people be the cause of so much trouble?

We spent the next hour watching Jews be compared to rats and cartoons of Jews with huge noses. We also saw pictures of the ideal German family, all blond haired and blue eyed, playing happily in the park. The movie was convincing. But because it was the Nazis saying it, I didn't want to believe it.

"Your homework tonight is to read the first two chapters of your racial textbook," Fräulein Haugen said at the end of that day's lessons. "It will help you to better understand the importance of race in Hitler's new world and to fully appreciate the Aryan ideal."

Franziska and Siegrid huddled on Siegrid's cot that evening, poring through the book together. They talked and giggled in places. I tried to concentrate on my book, ignoring the sounds coming from them. Watching them made my heart ache with loneliness for Terezie.

"Can I sit with you?" A voice interrupted my thoughts, and I looked up to find Liesel standing by my cot.

"Yes," I said, surprised. "Of course."

We spent a few minutes reading quietly to ourselves. The first few pages had graphs and charts about nose size and head width and lists of the specific physical standards for the true German ideal. In the pictures I recognized the metal instruments the doctors in the Kladno gym had used on me.

"No!" Liesel said out loud, then looked around to see if anyone besides me had heard her.

"Pardon?" I asked, looking over at her.

"This doesn't make sense to me." Her voice lowered to a whisper. "How can the size of your nose make any difference?"

I stared at her a few seconds before answering. I had been wondering the same thing but thought I was alone in my doubt. "You're right," I said, so quietly that only she could hear. "It makes no sense."

She smiled and continued to read. I smiled too, warmed by the thought that I might have found a friend.

✳

"Tell me what you learned from your studies last night," Fräulein Haugen demanded during class the next day. Immediately, many hands went into the air, and we spent the rest of the day discussing Hitler's views on race.

I had never been to school all year long. The late-summer air was hot and sticky and made it difficult to concentrate, especially when all we heard about was Germany, Germany, Germany. Constantly we were told of the glory of Germany, the glory of the Nazi party, the glory of Hitler. Constantly we were told that we were part of the German agenda. I had heard this so many times, it was hard to remember that I wasn't a Nazi, that I didn't want to be the Aryan ideal, that I hated Germany.

Perhaps that was what I had seen change in Franziska. Whereas I worked hard to remember that I was not German, Franziska seemed to embrace what she was learning. She studied even harder than she had in Lidice, and she appeared to accept everything that was told to her without question. It was as if she no longer remembered that she wasn't German.

One day, during lunch, Franziska and Gerde exploded into an argument. Loud shouts from the table brought Fräulein Krüger rushing over.

"What's this, girls? What is the meaning of this? Why these loud words?" A look of genuine concern was on her face. She sat down in an empty chair, pulling Franziska and Gerde into chairs on either side of her.

"Franziska says that my nose is not the right shape!" Gerde began, her lip quivering.

"There *are* certain standards for the Aryan nose," Franziska said with a sniff of authority, looking at Fräulein Krüger for approval.

"Oh, girls!" Fräulein Krüger laughed, putting an arm around each of them. "Franziska, I am glad you are concerned about the purity of our race, and Gerde, you need not worry. We can check."

She left the room and reappeared with the instrument I now understood was used to measure nose size. Carefully, she pressed it against each girl's nose.

"See, Gerde, yours is a bit longer than Franziska's," Fräulein Krüger noted, "but still within the correct limits." Gerde smiled.

"So, really, you are both right, and there is no need to argue. Now, everyone, off to afternoon lessons." Fräulein Krüger hurried us out of the room with a wave of her hand.

I walked toward our classroom behind Franziska and Gerde, who were chatting happily. Now that Fräulein Krüger had made it clear that Gerde's nose was acceptable, it seemed as if it was all right for Franziska to be friends with her.

"Noses again."

I turned to see Liesel walking next to me. "Pardon me?" I asked, not sure what she was talking about.

"Noses. That's what Franziska and Gerde were fussing over. What a ridiculous thing to argue about."

"I agree." I smiled, following Liesel into the classroom.

"Good. Then we won't have to measure our noses to see if we can be friends," she said, sliding into the chair next to me and winking at me.

✳

That afternoon we sat through a long, boring arithmetic lesson. The monotonous drone of the teacher, Fräulein Müller, was making it hard to concentrate. I had begun wearing Babichka's pin on the inside of my skirt, rather than my shirt, so that I could easily finger its outline during the day without being noticed. Now I felt for the pin through the pleats of my skirt and let my mind drift.

The warmth outside and the tedious sounds of the lecture made me think of the piano lessons

Mama had insisted I take the year before. Mama was very good at piano and singing and all things musical, and she had made me sit at the piano for hours in the warm summer air, practicing the same chords and scales over and over again. Unfortunately, I was clumsy and awkward, and her wish for me to play the piano well had been disappointed. I had found both the lessons and the practice pointless and tiring.

One hot summer day Papa and Jaro had appeared at the window as I sat practicing.

"Milada! Come here." Jaro beckoned from outside, his head appearing just above the windowsill. I stopped playing and put my hands in my lap.

"Jaro, what are you doing? I'm supposed to be practicing," I whispered. "Mama will be mad."

Papa's head appeared next to Jaro's, a grin on his face. "Your mama has left for tea with Mrs. Janecek."

I needed no further prompting and climbed out the window and into the arms of Papa and Jaro. We spent the next hour sitting in the field, watching clouds and chewing wheat gum. While we were there, I told Papa that I didn't really enjoy the piano. A few weeks later Mama announced suddenly that I didn't have to take piano lessons anymore, and even though he said nothing, I had had a feeling Papa had convinced her to let me stop.

Tears began to roll down my face as I thought of this time with Jaro and Papa. When would I see them again?

"And then . . ." Fräulein Müller stopped in mid-sentence, staring at me as the tears dripped from my chin. Everyone in class was suddenly awake and interested, turning to see what she was looking at. I straightened and desperately tried to stop the tears, afraid that I would receive a beating like Heidi.

Fräulein Müller walked to her desk and withdrew a handkerchief. "We must be careful to add the proper numbers to get the sum," she continued, dropping the handkerchief on my desk. "Of course, you know, there will be exceptions."

Tears were routine that first summer at the center. Some girls cried every moment they were awake. Others walked around with eyes that were dry but looked dazed and confused. Clean, fresh handkerchiefs were always available, but there was never any acknowledgment of our sadness, never a hug or a pat on the shoulder. In the eyes of our captors sadness was the same as weakness, and weakness would not be acknowledged or tolerated. We were, after all, Germany's hope and pride. We were the chosen Aryan nation, God's special children, sent to save the world from the Jews.

I was learning to tuck away pieces of my real self: the girl from Czechoslovakia who had a family waiting somewhere for her. I was learning to put that girl in a box during the day, safe and secure, until just before going to sleep at night. Then I could take the real girl out in the darkness and examine her more closely.

The days belonged to Hitler, but the nights were

mine. At night I could step inside my memories and listen to Mama singing our own beautiful national anthem, not the ugly German song I awoke to each morning. I could see Jaroslav and Papa playing ball and watch Terezie riding her bike. I could see Anechka's little hands playing patty-cake and Babichka's nimble fingers kneading the morning bread. If I tried hard enough, I could even see Babichka's face: her hair in the bun she always wore and the plain dresses she liked, with their tiny flowers sprinkled across the fabric. But it was getting harder to hear her laugh or remember the sound of her voice.

✵

By October we had been at the center for four months, and it seemed Franziska was starting to forget her real self. *Really* forget. Not just tucking away who she was, but erasing everything she had been before coming to the center. As hard as I worked to remember, it seemed, Franziska worked to forget.

She excelled in everything and had become the shining example of the ideal Aryan girl. In the few short months since we'd been at the center, she had grown taller and more confident. She was an eager participant in all parts of our training and seemed to be slipping further and further away from the person she had been in Lidice.

Heidi, however, continued to struggle. Her problems worsened after the beating she received from Fräulein Schmitt. It was as though she was caving in on herself a little bit each day, and nothing seemed to help.

Her sister, Elsa, stayed protectively by her side, constantly reminding Heidi what she should be doing and where she should be going. She tutored Heidi in German at night, going over the day's lessons with her long after the lights were off and everyone else had grown quiet. But Heidi seemed to wilt a little more each day. She grew thin and walked around looking dazed and lost. Several times she wet her bed. One night we awoke to the hushed sounds of Elsa moving about in the darkened room.

"What is it?" Franziska asked, pushing herself up to lean on one elbow.

"I think Heidi wet the bed again," I whispered.

"She shouldn't drink so much water before going to sleep." Franziska sat all the way up.

"Would you like help, Elsa?" It was Gerde, from the other side of the room.

"No, no. Just go back to sleep," Elsa replied, her voice tense and quick. In the dark I could see her outline as she removed the covering from Heidi's cot and tried to air it out.

The next morning Fräulein Krüger knew what had happened the minute she walked in.

"Again, Heidi?" she asked, her lips pursed together so tightly that the words coming through them sounded like the hiss of a snake.

Heidi nodded, her eyes on the floor. Everyone was standing in the morning pose, arms out in the

Hitler salute, waiting to be dismissed for breakfast.

"Well, Heidi. Well, well." Without finishing the morning inspection, Fräulein Krüger left the room, clicking her tongue and absently waving a hand behind her to release us from our salute.

The next afternoon neither Heidi nor Elsa appeared for lessons.

"Heidi needs additional training," Fräulein Krüger announced, interrupting our last lesson that day. "She will attend a special camp for this training."

Franziska glanced at me with an I-told-you-so look on her face. I was filled with a jealousy so strong, I could feel the hair on my arms raise. Perhaps Heidi had been sent back home, and was with her mama and papa by now.

"I knew something would *have* to be done," Franziska murmured next to me. The superior look was still on her face. "I am sure it is a good camp."

When we returned to our bunks after lessons, Heidi's cot was gone. Elsa sat on her own cot, the one that had been next to her sister's, with a handkerchief wound between her fingers. Her eyes were red and swollen.

"Oh, Elsa. Don't worry." Gerde went to her and put an arm around her shoulder. "She will come back once she's learned what she needs to."

"No." Elsa said flatly. "No. She will not." My stomach gave a lurch at the finality of those words. Suddenly, I felt guilty for my jealousy earlier.

For the next two days Elsa refused to get out of bed or participate in anything. At first Fräulein Krüger was kind and understanding, as she tried to coax Elsa back into our daily routine. But by the third day she was losing patience, and on the fourth she resorted to a beating. All of us stood in our morning salute listening to the German national anthem on the invisible phonograph, as Fräulein Krüger hit Elsa with a leather belt. The sounds of the belt mixed with the tinny chords of the music, but Elsa made no sound at all. She just lay in bed, receiving strike after strike.

The next day Elsa, too, was gone. We were told she had been sent to the same place that Heidi had gone for "additional training." With a bright smile Fräulein Krüger assured us that both girls would come back as soon as they were ready. But somehow, deep in my heart, I knew that wasn't true.

Late into the night, long after the lights had been turned off, we discussed this from our cots.

"Maybe they were sent home?" Gerde whispered hopefully.

There was a grunt from Franziska. "Fräulein Krüger said they were sent to a camp for additional training."

Several murmurs of agreement came from across the room.

"What if they were shot? I've seen that happen. Once, in Poland," Siegrid whispered from her cot.

"Oh, Siegrid, don't think such thoughts. I don't

exactly know what happened, but I am sure they are safe." This came from Gerde.

"I saw someone shot once too. Right out in the open. A Jew." Ilse spoke up from her cot. "They do shoot people."

"Jews deserve to be shot," Franziska interrupted.

I winced and heard Liesel gasp beside me. It was such a cold statement. Fräulein Krüger would have been proud.

"Just go to sleep. Don't talk of such things. Everyone just go to sleep," whispered Gerde.

I lay awake for a long time after that. Fräulein Krüger had said Heidi and Elsa had gone to a camp. She had assured us everything was fine. But she was also the one who said my town had come under attack by the Allies, and I knew that was not true.

I tried to put the sisters out of my mind and finally fell into a restless sleep.

five

By January we had been in the center for seven months. The air outside was cold, and the short skirts of our uniforms had been replaced with long, itchy woolen ones. Each of us had a lined winter coat, complete with the Nazi eagle sewn on the collar, and a pair of warm winter boots.

Routine settled over the center like a thick blanket, covering everything in dull, lifeless shades of gray. Day after day was the same. Even the food that had once seemed so wonderful now tasted plain and dreary to my tongue.

Every morning began with the German national anthem and our salute to Hitler, then calisthenics and German lessons. In the afternoon there was more saluting, history and math lessons, and dinner. Then finally bedtime arrived, when I had a brief moment to think about my family, until I fell asleep and the same routine would begin again in a few short hours.

One night, just as I was drifting to sleep, Liesel's voice brought me fully awake.

"That is not so." She was arguing with Siegrid, whose cot was on her left. Liesel's voice was loud and angry.

"Yes, it is true," Siegrid replied. "You heard what Fräulein Krüger told us. Your mama doesn't want you anymore. You were too expensive. That is why no one has come for you."

"I am sure that if Fräulein Krüger said that, it is the truth," Franziska added from her own cot.

"No! That is *not* true. It's not." Liesel turned her back to Siegrid and faced me. Doubt and confusion rested in her eyes.

By that time almost everyone had stopped asking Fräulein Krüger or the other guards about their parents. The story was always the same. We were orphans from Allied air raids. Or we had become too expensive for our families. No matter which story was told, the end was always the same. We had been chosen to serve Hitler. We were Aryan girls of Germany. We were the hope of the future.

Secretly, I was glad no one asked much about their families anymore. Every time I heard the story that Lidice had been bombed by Allies, there was a small part of me that was actually starting to believe it. I could almost feel the vibrations of the bombs as they fell. It was easier to imagine that than to remember how I had been taken in the middle of the night by Nazis.

I lay awake, listening to the sound of Liesel crying.

"Liesel," I whispered. "Do you want to talk?"

"No, Eva. Go to sleep."

I looked around in the darkness. Moonlight was coming from the four small windows that lined one wall. To my right Franziska's eyelashes caught the light, and I could see she was also awake.

"Liesel," I continued softly. "You know what Siegrid said is not true. You know someday this will end and you will go home. We will all go home."

"What if Mama doesn't want me? What if it is true?"

Her questions brought tears to my eyes. "You have to think about what you do remember, Liesel. You have to hold on to that."

"I didn't even get to see my sisters to say goodbye. Mama was the only one home when they came for me. It was so awful. I will never forget the sound of her crying. Never."

"I remember my mama too. I try to think about her every night," I said. My finger traced the outline of Babichka's pin underneath my nightdress. "I think of everyone in my family every night."

"Oh, I'm sorry, Eva." Liesel's voice softened. "At least I know my mama is safe. It's so awful how your family was killed in an air raid."

"There was no air raid," I said. The words came out louder than I had intended.

"What?" she asked.

"There was no air raid," I repeated, needing to hear the words again myself. "We were taken in the middle of the night by Hitler's soldiers."

"But Fräulein Krüger said . . ." Liesel's voice held both doubt and hope.

"We were taken. In the middle of the night. By Hitler's soldiers," I repeated, highlighting each word carefully in the cold darkness.

The images of my last night in Lidice appeared vividly in my mind. I could see Papa's face, his hand outstretched toward Mama's as they were pulled apart. His eyes had been filled with a pain I had never seen before. I could still smell the sweet sourness of the hay as we waited for hours and days in the gym, and I could see my own hand outstretched toward Mama's as I was carried away.

Now I threw off my blankets in fury. Franziska sat up in her cot.

I turned to her. "You remember. You were there. You were taken too."

"No." Franziska's voice was soft and sure. It stung me as hard as Fräulein Krüger had when she had slapped me my first day at the center.

"What?" I was on my feet, anger making my head throb. "What do you mean *no*? How do you not remember? The soldiers, the guns, the trucks, the gym! What are you saying?"

"My family is dead." Her voice sounded strange, as if her throat had become too small for her words. I felt cold as all the anger left my body in a sudden rush. "They were killed in an Allied air raid on our town," Franziska continued.

Before I could reply, she lay down with her back to me and curled her blanket around her, leaving me to stand alone and shivering in the moonlight.

"Eva?" It was Liesel. "Eva?" she repeated.

I didn't look at her. "Good night, Liesel." I crawled into bed, hiding myself under the thick blanket.

"Good night," she said softly.

I lay on my cot, running one finger over and around Babichka's little star pin. It was the only thing I had from my home.

I thought of my last night in Lidice and the beautiful telescope Papa had given me for my birthday. Was someone looking at the stars through it at this moment?

I remembered the night Terezie and I had been planning my party, discussing the songs we were going to sing and the games we were going to play. And we had been gazing at the stars. *Eva, look.* Terezie had said, pointing at a shooting star as it streaked across the sky.

No, something wasn't right. I ran my mind back over the memory. Terezie had said, *Look.* But she had not used the name Eva. What had she called me?

Butterflies fluttered softly in my stomach. There

was an empty spot where my name should be, like the hole left in your mouth after you lose a tooth. For a long time I lay in the dark, running my mind over and around the hole, trying to remember what I had been called before coming to this place. But no name would come.

Over the next few weeks the hole grew into a thick fog, clouding everything I did. I tried to smile and nod and continue with lessons and exercises and routines so that I would not be sent away like Heidi and Elsa. But every night I would touch Babichka's pin and search for my name, growing a little sadder each time I could not find it.

I thought of her words as she gave me the pin. *Remember who you are,* she had whispered. *Remember where you are from. Always.*

I had broken my promise to her.

Several weeks later I was awakened during the night by a sudden sharp pain in my leg. Babichka's pin had come open beneath my nightdress and was sticking me. I took it off and held it in my hand as I listened to the rhythmic breathing of the other girls mix with the scraping sound of wind blowing bits of snow against the windows.

Snow had come to rest permanently on the ground, signaling that winter had found its way to us. We could see our breath in the morning when we did outdoor calisthenics, and hot cocoa had become a regular part of our meals.

I traced Babichka's pin, touching each tiny garnet, and pictured my grandmother that last day with her fingers wrapped around mine. I searched again for my name, trying to find it in the crystals, hoping it was not lost forever.

I turned and looked through the little window on the other side of Franziska. Frost covered the lower part of the pane, and only the smallest bit of night sky peeked into the room from the top. I squinted into the small space of blackness, trying to catch a glimpse of any stars.

I needed to see the stars, to look up into their light as I had done so many times in Lidice. For several minutes I listened for the sounds of the night guard. Hearing nothing, I quietly put on my boots and coat, crept down the hall, and slipped outside.

The night was crisp and beautiful, the sky dotted with thousands of stars. Amazed, I stretched as high as I could. The stars in Poland looked exactly like those in Czechoslovakia! Somewhere, perhaps at that very moment, my family was looking at those same stars. I found the North Star and stared at it, as if I was looking through a telescope, searching for a glimpse of my name.

Suddenly, a tiny streak of light raced across the sky. Then another. And another. Shooting stars! The sky filled briefly with them. Babichka! It had to be a message from my grandmother, telling me to remember, remember who I was.

I started crying, the tears freezing almost immediately on my face.

Sleep, my little one, sleep.
The angels watch over you.

I remembered the soft, sweet words of the lullaby Babichka used to sing to me. It filled my head in the darkness, and I closed my eyes, humming softly, tracing her pin with my finger.

And then, I remembered what Babichka called me as she sang this lullaby. I remembered my name.

Sleep, my Milada, sleep.
All the whole night through.

Milada. My fingers touched my name, my beautiful sweet name. *Milada.* The name that belonged to my grandmother and her mother before her.

Milada. There it was, lovely and pure and real.

"I won't forget," I whispered out loud as the streaks of light faded. "Babichka, I won't forget."

Milada, Milada, Milada, I promised, as I made my way back to the sleeping room.

⁂

Remembering my name brought bits of color back into the center, lifting an edge of the gray blanket that had settled over everything. It was a little easier to do home economics lessons and a little less difficult to look at Hitler's face every day because I knew, beneath everything, who I was and where I belonged. And even though Franziska didn't believe it, I knew someday I would go back to my village and live in my house with my family and be called by my real name again.

This was all the knowledge I needed to help warm the winter and make the center and the daily lessons more bearable.

Not long after I had remembered my name, Fräulein Haugen brought a full-length mirror to a health lesson. Each of us was weighed, and had her heart checked and her head and nose once again measured. Then, one by one, we were brought to the mirror, where Fräulein Haugen showed us how to style our hair into an intricate twist.

I had not looked into a mirror since coming to the center, and the person who stared back at me from the glass was someone I did not know. I put a hand up to my face, and the girl in the mirror did the same. My hair had grown past my shoulders, and my face had changed as well. It was longer, and the freckles had faded. The person in the mirror looked less like a little girl and more like a young woman.

I peered at the blond hair and blue eyes, things I had never paid attention to before, things that had changed me from a Czech girl into a future German citizen.

✻

A month further into winter, I awoke again in the middle of the night. From someplace far away I could hear Babichka's Czech lullaby, beautiful and pure, floating in my ears. But someone was trying to shake it out of me.

I opened my eyes. Liesel stood above my cot, shaking my shoulders gently.

"Eva. Eva? What are you doing?" she whispered in German. "You're singing and I can't understand you. Wake up. Wake up!"

"What?" I asked in Czech.

"Eva, wake up! I can't understand what you are saying."

"I am awake," I whispered in German, disappointed to realize where I was. I wanted to fade back into the warmth of the song. Pieces of it still floated in my mind like soft feathers.

I sat up and looked into Liesel's eyes. Even in the darkness, with only the moonlight to see by, their blue color was striking. I patted a spot on my cot, and she joined me, curling her legs up under her nightdress and wrapping her arms around her knees. We sat for a long while in silence, listening to the breathing of the other girls.

"You have the prettiest eyes, Liesel," I whispered.

"Thank you," she said. "They're just like my mother's. . . ." She stopped and turned away.

I looked at Franziska's sleeping form beside me as I thought about Liesel. She was the first person who had smiled at me after coming to the center. Her eyes were the only pretty thing I had seen.

What had she been like before coming to this

place? Had she been someone I would have liked or someone I wouldn't have wanted at my birthday party, like Franziska? How had this place changed Liesel? How had this place changed me?

I stood and paused to hear if any of the other girls were awake or if the night guard was near. Liesel looked up at me, and I held out my hand to her.

"Come," I whispered, when I was sure no one else was awake. Quietly I led us down the narrow aisle between the two rows of cots to where our coats and boots were stored. I pulled mine on and motioned for Liesel to do the same. She didn't hesitate but followed what I was doing without question. Together we slipped outside through the small door near the sleeping room and into the cold darkness.

Twinkling stars filled the sky. Our teacher in Czechoslovakia had once told us that stars are really like suns: giant balls of heat and light, and not the tiny shining crystals we see when we look up.

Liesel huddled close behind me, shivering in her coat and trying to see the path beneath her so she wouldn't stumble.

"Look!" I stopped and pointed. "Look! That's the North Star. Do you see it? It's always in the sky, no matter what the season. Even here the stars are the same."

She followed the direction where I pointed and nodded. "Stars," she whispered. "I guess I had never noticed."

We stood for several minutes watching the stars

blink randomly, as if each one had its own rhythm.

Liesel began shivering, and I too could feel the cold trying to slip into my coat. I wasn't sure why I had wanted to bring Liesel outside, but I wasn't ready to return to the sleeping room either. On a sudden impulse, I pulled her toward the little church, which we saw every day but which I had never entered. I hoped the door was not locked and that we could find warmth there.

The wooden door was old and heavy, much like the door on our church in Lidice, but it opened easily. Inside, everything was dark except for the altar, which was decorated with League of German Girls posters and adorned with a large picture of the Führer. Dozens of tiny red candles burned in little glasses beneath the picture, the flames flickering like the stars outside. Near Hitler's picture stood a statue of the Virgin Mary. The expression on her face seemed mournful, as if she was sad to see the changes in the church.

I walked slowly to the front of the church, feeling the smooth, worn wood of each pew with my bare fingers. Liesel stood at the back of the church with her arms wrapped around herself. She looked unsure of what to do next.

"This is a Catholic church, yes?" she asked quietly in the darkness.

"It used to be. Yes," I answered.

"Are you Catholic?" she asked. "I mean, I guess . . . were you Catholic? Before coming here?"

"Yes," I answered. "And you?"

She nodded, adding, "But I don't think this church is Catholic any longer."

I shook my head. "They have turned it into something ugly. I think this used to be a convent. But now, it is . . ." I stopped, unable to think of words to describe what it had been turned into. "Evil."

Liesel found a pew in the middle of the church and sat down. I went and sat next to her. Even though the air in the church was warmer than outside, it was still cold and we could see our breath. We sat without speaking until she broke the silence.

"Katarzyna," she whispered.

"What did you say?" I asked, turning to look at her.

"Katarzyna. That is my real name. That was my name before I was brought here."

A shiver, not caused by cold, ran through me. I wasn't the only one who hadn't forgotten about life before this place. "Oh, Liesel . . . I mean, Katarzyna! My name is Milada."

"Milada. That is a pretty name."

"I say it to myself every night. So I won't forget."

We sat together for a while, just watching the eerie face of Hitler wavering in the shadows.

"I have something I want to show you," I said. Unbuttoning my coat, I reached beneath my night-dress skirt and unclasped Babichka's star pin. Carefully, I pulled it out and pressed it into her hand. "The night I was taken from my home, my grandmother gave this to me. She said to remember. Remember, always."

Liesel looked at the pin, then back at me. "You are lucky to have something from home. I have nothing. I wasn't allowed to bring anything."

"I have tried to keep my promise to remember."

She handed the pin back to me.

"Katarzyna?" I asked.

She smiled. "Yes, Milada."

"Let's make another promise. When we are here, in this church, let's use our real names."

"Yes, Milada," she answered, grasping my hand.

"Good, then, Katarzyna." I smiled back at her, squeezing her hand in mine.

"My name is Milada. Milada!" I said it so loudly that the sound bounced off the church walls in an echo. She laughed.

"Katarzyna!" she yelled, letting the name roll down the pews.

We sat for a long time in the church, looking at Hitler's face and the faint glow of the candles. Even with the cold, I felt warmed by the knowledge that I had a friend. I wasn't alone after all.

six

At the same time that I was finding a friend in Liesel, Franziska was growing close to Siegrid. The two became inseparable. They sat together in every class and at every meal. They made a special request to have their cots in the sleeping room moved next to each other. And they would whisper late into the night back and forth in flawless German.

Both continued to excel at German history and language lessons. Both were model German citizens: eager, smart, always prepared, and quick to criticize anyone who faltered in the slightest way, either in lessons or in her allegiance to the Nazis.

Fräulein Krüger and the other instructors pointed them out as examples of young German women who "have the best handwriting" or "truly understand the German philosophy" or "will become fine German mothers someday."

Everyone else seemed either jealous of them or irritated by the constant praise they received. But we were all too afraid of what Fräulein Krüger or the other adults would do if we openly defied or challenged either girl.

Franziska was the teachers' favorite because she so completely embraced the Nazi philosophy of the adults around her. And she not only knew she had this power, she also knew how to use it.

One day, during a lesson, Franziska was reciting a passage from a German poem. We had all worked hard the night before in the sleeping room, reading the assigned lines back and forth to one another, trying to memorize them. Franziska, of course, had memorized the poem quickly and seemingly effortlessly, while the rest of us had struggled.

I wasn't surprised when Fräulein Schmitt called on Franziska to recite the first part of the poem. She delivered it perfectly, and Fräulein Schmitt lavished praise on her.

"Now, Franziska, you may pick a partner to recite the second half with you, in unison."

There was no hesitation from Franziska. "I would like to recite with Gerde."

Gerde's face reddened. We all knew she had struggled most of all to memorize the poem.

"All right, Gerde," Fräulein Schmitt said. "You and Franziska may begin."

It was painful to listen as Gerde attempted to keep up with Franziska's pace and confidence.

Franziska kept having to stop so that Gerde could check her book for a forgotten line. When they finished, Gerde's eyes were filled with tears.

"Franziska, that was beautiful," Fräulein Schmitt said, clapping her hands together. "You are always so excellent with your studies. And Gerde, I don't think I need to tell you how poor your performance was. To be a proper German girl, you must study as hard as Franziska does, even if it means less sleep at night. Tonight you will not go to bed with the other girls. Instead, you will sit with the night guard in this classroom until you have learned to recite this poem as well as Franziska."

Everyone studied harder the next time we had a poem to memorize. All of us were willing to forgo sleep because we were so afraid Franziska would use her power to humiliate us.

✳

I was glad that I had Liesel. We continued to make periodic visits to the church at night. One of us would stay awake and then awaken the other after everyone else was sleeping soundly. Together we would sneak out into the night to look up at the stars and sit in the small church and talk. These visits were what kept hope alive and made the center bearable throughout that second year.

Inside the church we created our own place with our own rules. We called each other by our real names and talked about things from before. I told Katarzyna about my family, about Jaro and

Anechka and Mama and Papa and Babichka. I let her hold Babichka's pin, and I described how Babichka had taught me to sew and bake. I told her about Terezie and the things we had done together and the birthday party we had planned but never had. Our time together felt comfortable and real, like the moments I had spent with Terezie. And I began to consider Katarzyna, like Terezie, a best friend.

"I have three older sisters and an older brother," she said one night, after I had told her about Jaroslav being so nice to me at my birthday party. "Father was killed fighting the Nazis when I was still little, and my brother hates them because of that. And yet here I am, one of them."

"But you're not a Nazi," I told her. "Not really."

"I know. But sometimes it is hard to remember." We sat in the dark for a few minutes before she continued.

"They came for me, you know. The Nazis. They just walked up to the door, came in, and took me with them. I guess that's why I don't really believe that Mother willingly gave me to them. I'll never forget the way she cried and screamed as they pulled me from her."

I nodded, and she continued.

"They were wearing brown uniforms, and on the bus they told me that mama could no longer afford me and had given me to them freely. I don't think that's true. I was the youngest in the family and didn't eat much. But sometimes, in here, it's hard to know the truth. . . ."

Her voice trailed off, and I squeezed her hand.

※

As the winter turned to spring, our friendship became easy and familiar, something certain in a place filled with so much uncertainty. I had nearly outgrown another woolen skirt by then, and my boots barely fit. My hair hung far below my shoulders, and my stockings had become so tight that they had to be replaced for a third time.

One morning I awoke to the strains of the German national anthem mixed with the sound of birds chattering, announcing that spring might have finally arrived. The birds' song made me feel lighthearted and happy, ready for the warmth of spring.

When Fräulein Krüger came to inspect us that morning, she wore a formal jacket instead of her regular shirt and dress scarf. We stood at attention as usual while she walked up and down the narrow aisle, smiling and nodding her approval. Out of the corner of my eye I could see Franziska's gaze following her eagerly, as if Fräulein Krüger was a movie star.

I thought of the real movie stars Terezie and I used to discuss together. We were sure they were not only beautiful but kind and generous as well. Our dream was that one would come to Lidice someday and whisk us away in an expensive car for a fancy meal in Prague. How different from this Fräulein Krüger was.

She did look beautiful that morning. Her hair was tightly gathered in a silky gold bun at the back of her head. This accentuated her eyes, which were a dark shade of blue that reminded me of the color of the sky right before a thunderstorm. And like thunderclouds, I knew, they hid something ugly just beneath their surface, waiting for its chance to be free.

"You look good this morning, my girls!" Her voice was unusually cheerful, making me even more suspicious of her intentions. "And today, young women of Germany, you will take your first trip into the town of Puschkau."

The room filled with a stunned silence as Fräulein Krüger continued walking up and down the aisle. She patted a head here and touched a cheek there, then released us from our salute and left the room, humming.

No one spoke as we watched her leave. Together we walked the short distance to the dining room, and still no one spoke. Liesel and I exchanged nervous glances but said nothing.

I hadn't thought of Heidi in a long time, but images of her last day filled my mind. I could still hear the sound of Fräulein Krüger's belt on Elsa's skin before she too had gone. Were we really going to town? Or were we being sent away, as they had been?

Sensing our unease, Fräulein Krüger joined us for breakfast and sat at the head of the long dining table. "Girls, girls. This will be fun. A way to show off your beauty. And besides, we have a surprise for you." I looked down at my oatmeal, trying to make my throat swallow. I had come to hate surprises during the past two years.

Milada, Milada, Milada, I said to myself, letting the syllables dance in my head in time to my chewing.

After breakfast, Fräulein Krüger led us back to the sleeping room instead of taking us to home economics lessons. I noticed, with a sense of dread, that the door was closed. I glanced at Liesel and saw by the expression on her face that she was also frightened. What surprise lay behind that door?

Fräulein Krüger gathered us closely around her in a small circle and opened the door with a flourish. "I have something special for you." With a wide smile she swept her arm toward the cots. "When in town, you should look like the beautiful German girls you are. Please change, and then we can depart."

On each of our cots lay a brand-new, neatly pressed formal uniform, the fabric looking crisp and inviting. At the foot of each cot was a pair of shiny patent leather shoes, so new that I thought I could actually smell them from the door.

Tears came unexpectedly. It had been so long since I had been given a gift. All the fear drained from me, making my knees weak. We were really going to town.

I watched Liesel take her skirt and hold it up against her legs to check the length. She smiled at me, turning the skirt around, then holding it against her legs again.

"Look. It's perfect!" she said.

Everyone's tension disappeared, and the room filled with excited cries as we pulled on our new clothes. My shirt fit as if it had been made just for me. The fabric was thick and rich and obviously expensive. There was a red kerchief for my neck, with a new Nazi clasp that was similar to the ones for our daily uniforms. Carefully, I took Grandmother's star and pinned it underneath the skirt.

Liesel stood next to me, twirling in her skirt. "Did you look yet? In the pocket? See what they have given us?"

I put my hand in my pocket and gasped as my fingers closed around a small object. I pulled it out to see a coin, a bronze-colored German mark, with the Nazi eagle and swastika stamped on one side. A whole mark, one for each of us, in the pocket of each skirt.

Fräulein Krüger appeared at the door again, a genuine smile of pleasure on her face. "The marks, young women, are for you to spend in whatever way you wish. We will stop at a special candy stand during our trip into town."

Never had I had so much money to spend on my own. Never. And I couldn't remember the last time I had visited a candy stand, let alone been allowed to buy a sweet. Twirling in my own skirt, I closed my eyes and let the smile stay on my face.

❉

The day was sunny and warm as we made our way to the bus. As I walked, I realized it would be the first time I had been away from the center in nearly two years. What would the world outside look like? Would it have changed, or would it look the same?

Small patches of leftover snow lay melting on the ground, and the mountains in the distance were outlined in a hazy light blue that matched Liesel's eyes. Birds were singing gloriously in the few trees that dotted the center. Franziska and Siegrid babbled excitedly all the way to the bus, and Liesel caught up to me, putting her hand in mine. She had tied a new ribbon in her hair, and the sun caught the color of her eyes, making them even brighter than usual. Everything about the whole world felt right and good at that moment.

The Polish foothills moved past us through the bus window as we drove to town. I had a fleeting memory of the last time I had traveled this route two years before, but I pushed it aside. I wanted to enjoy the freedom of being gone from the center for as long as possible without reliving dark memories.

The world outside looked beautiful and clean, as if there was no war, no center, no need to remember who you were. I pressed my forehead against the cool window and watched the scenery pass until we entered the town of Puschkau.

The buildings were different from any I had seen before. They were close together and looked sad and dark. They stood huddled next to one another, as if they too needed to protect themselves against Hitler and his occupation.

Despite the buildings, I felt lighthearted and happy, almost joyful. We were allowed to wander in and among the shops, and Liesel and I walked together, giggling and talking. I kept my mark safely in my pocket, unwilling to spend it on anything but chocolate. I was happy just to be outside and free, like the birds chattering in the trees.

Our last stop was a group visit to the small candy stand near the bus. All of us met and walked together, a group of blond German girls strolling down the street without a care.

"Sweets. I can hardly wait!" Liesel whispered to me as we walked side by side. Her eyes were shining.

"Sweets," I repeated, my mouth watering at the thought, my mind trying to remember the rich taste of chocolate candy.

At the stand I chose a small piece of chocolate with a little rose carved on top. I put it in my mouth and closed my eyes, letting it melt without biting it, to make the taste linger as long as possible.

When I opened my eyes, I saw an old, bent woman standing across the street, looking in my direction.

"Grandmother," I whispered.

For a moment I was sure it *was* my grandmother, standing across the street in Poland, waiting for me to go to her. Suddenly, the only thing that mattered was having her wrap me in her ragged black shawl so I could feel her and smell her and listen to her tell me that everything was going to be all right. My whole body ached with longing, and I reached a hand out to her.

But as I moved toward her, she screamed at me in words I couldn't understand. Her eyes were clouded with hate—black and smoky, like hot coals from a fire. She shouted at me again, loud and hoarse, opening her toothless mouth. "Nazista!" she screamed in Polish. Then in broken German: "Nazi! Evil child!" In a moment, she had crossed the street and was standing so close to me that I could smell her earthy sweat and feel the heat of her words.

"No," I said, wanting her to know I wasn't a Nazi. I looked down at my clothes, suddenly feeling ashamed. "No," I repeated, shaking my head. I wanted to rip my uniform off. She didn't understand. I wasn't a Nazi.

Slowly she pursed her lips together, then spat at me and watched with satisfaction as the spit rolled down my cheek and onto the sidewalk. She smiled, eyes still burning, and straightened her back, making herself as tall as she could.

"No," I said again, wiping the spit from my face. "I . . ." I reached out to touch her, but suddenly Fräulein Krüger was between us, with a billy club in her hand that she lifted over her head and brought down hard on the woman. Again and again Fräulein Krüger struck her—on her head, her arms, her back—until the old woman lay on the ground. Her screams, loud at first, lessened with each blow, until they finally stopped altogether, and I heard only the sound of Fräulein Krüger's stick on the woman's body. For days afterward I would awake in the middle of the night to the sounds of the old woman's screams mixed with the dull thump of Fräulein Krüger's club.

With brisk efficiency Fräulein Krüger hurried us all toward the bus. I turned one last time to see the woman slowly lifting herself from the ground. The snow around her was blotched with red. The streets were empty.

"Nasty old woman." Franziska appeared beside me in the aisle of the bus, patting my shoulder. "Nasty, nasty woman."

Clucking sympathetically, Fräulein Krüger took out a handkerchief and wiped the side of my face where the old woman had spit. Liesel stood on my other side, patting my back.

"It's nothing to worry over, Eva. She was a crazy old woman," Gerde said as we walked down the aisle.

"She got what she deserved," Siegrid agreed. "Everything is as it should be."

I sat down, surrounded by the murmurs of the girls, and the bus started with a lurch. I felt shaky and cold all over.

"Eva, are you all right?" Franziska chose a seat next to me, suddenly my good friend.

"That woman. That old woman. She thought I was a Nazi," I whispered.

"You are a Nazi," Franziska replied.

I looked at her. I saw her long hair held loosely in

a braid and noticed her strong cheekbones. Fräulein Krüger had praised Franziska once for the structure of her face. "A perfect Nazi face," she had said.

"But . . . no . . . ," I began.

"No, Eva. Stop." Franziska covered my hand with her own. "We are all safe."

I turned toward the window and wished I could get back the feeling I'd had on the drive into town. But all that happiness was gone, replaced by the harshness of where I was and whom I was with.

"She looked like my grandmother," I whispered softly, watching the trees and foothills as we drove back to the center.

Something in me changed after that. I felt as though I slipped a little farther away from everyone around me, even Liesel. Our daytime routine remained the same—lessons, Hitler, and Germany, Germany, Germany—and Liesel and I kept up our nighttime visits, but something was different.

I continued to keep my promise, *Milada, Milada, Milada*, and I continued to listen and wait and hope. But there seemed to be a gap between me and the rest of the world, and I didn't know how to cross it.

seven

April 1944: Puschkau, Poland

A few weeks after the trip to town, our early-morning routine was interrupted again.

This time Fräulein Krüger said nothing, offering no hints of surprises or good news. No new clothes awaited us. The only sign that something was different was that Fräulein Krüger wore her formal Nazi uniform. It was decorated with medals and draped with a sash that read *The League of German Girls*.

Instead of going to home economics lessons after breakfast, we were taken as a group to the little church that Liesel and I had spent so many nights visiting.

"Do you think we're going back to town?" asked Siegrid, as we were directed into the church.

"Oh, I hope so. I hope we get to stop at the candy stand again," said Gerde.

Liesel walked beside me. "What do you think is going on?" she asked.

"I don't know," I said nervously.

In the daylight I could see that bright white paint covered the walls of the church, and an even larger picture of the Führer had replaced the one that was usually above the altar. A large League of German Girls poster hung where the statue of Mary had been, and small red candles burned brightly everywhere. On either side of the Führer dozens of blood-red roses were arranged in crystal vases.

Liesel slid into the pew, sitting next to me. "It looks different in the day, doesn't it?" she whispered.

I nodded, and she patted my arm and looked toward the front. Whispers and giggles from the other girls filled the church.

"Heil Hitler!" The church fell silent as Fräulein Krüger appeared from a side door with two male Nazi guards I had never seen before. They were dressed in uniforms that were decorated with medals, and they wore polished black boots. A fresh wave of nervousness clenched my stomach.

"Heil Hitler!" I jumped up with everyone in salute.

"You may be seated." Fräulein Krüger approached the podium at the front of the church. Her hair was braided and wound around the back of her head in a way that reminded me of a spiderweb. So much poison under all that beauty.

"Today, German girls, is a most special day," she began.

The war is over. That was the first wild and hopeful thought that jumped into my head. The war is over and I am going back to Mama and Papa to be called by my real name and have a party with real cake and all of this will be forgotten as if it was a bad dream.

"Today you begin your new lives as official German citizens." She saluted the two male officers in the front row as they stood.

All the feeling drained from my body. The war was not over. The nightmare would continue.

"Your training has been difficult, I know," Fräulein Krüger continued, "but you have become fine young German girls. Girls we are proud to say will one day belong to Hitler's League of German Girls. And today ..." She stopped briefly, addressing her smile toward each of us in turn. "Today you will be adopted into your new German families."

For a moment the whole world became nothing but blank, empty space. Everything froze, like a clock that suddenly stops ticking. And just as quickly the church and the pews and Fräulein Krüger's voice started spinning and faded away into soft velvet blackness.

When I opened my eyes, two strangers stood over me. It was quiet. Too quiet. I felt dizzy when I tried to sit up, and a woman's hand gently pushed me down again. I was on my cot in the sleeping room, and a pretty woman I had never seen before was smiling down at me. A man stood near her, frowning and studying me through bushy eyebrows. Fräulein Krüger was off to the side, speaking rapidly.

"... part of the excitement. She is a strong girl, I assure you. She stood up to an attack by a Pole."

The woman stroked my forehead with her hand, the way Mama used to when I was sick, and I closed my eyes again. "Of course. Of course." She had a soft, gentle voice, musical and sweet. "Everything is fine now, Eva. We are ready to welcome you into our family."

✳

We pulled away from the center in an official Nazi car. Its black color shone like oil.

Fräulein Krüger stood on the church steps, smiling and waving, as we drove away from the place I had called home for nearly two years. It occurred to me that I had not seen Liesel or any of the other girls before I left. I had not even had a chance to say good-bye.

I was certain Fräulein Krüger would know where Liesel was, and I had to fight the urge to jump out of the car and run back. I had spent two years being afraid of Fräulein Krüger, and now I was genuinely afraid to leave her. But all I could do was watch her grow smaller and smaller through the rear window of the car until we turned a corner and she disappeared altogether.

I was alone with these strangers.

The dense brush of the Polish landscape moved

past, slowly at first and then gaining speed as we traveled along the main road. My new parents sat with me in the backseat while their chauffeur drove.

Outside the car, spring was making a full appearance. Tiny buds dotted the trees, looking as if they were ready to burst into bloom. Inside the car, the pretty woman talked nervously. But I kept my gaze fixed out the window, feeling numb and disconnected and not really hearing what she was saying. The man said nothing.

"... so happy to have you with us. We know it must have been traumatic, the air raid and the circumstances that brought you to us. You can call me Mutter."

Her words drifted in and out of my ears. *Milada, Milada, Milada,* I thought.

"And your friend Franziska. . . . Fräulein Krüger told us you were close and that her family was also lost in the air raid. She is being adopted by the Schönfelders, just a darling family. They live in Berlin. You two can certainly write to each other, and we might even be able to arrange a visit."

The trees rushed past, their branches whispering to me: *Milada, Milada, Milada.*

"We have a dog, Kaiser. He's the sweetest German shepherd. And you have a little brother, Peter, who is eight. And you will just love Elsbeth. She is fourteen, and she can't wait to have a sister."

"Let her rest, Trude. Let her rest." The father, Hans Werner, stopped her endless chatter. "It's been a long day for everyone."

I looked away from the window and met the woman's eyes briefly. My new mother, Trude Werner, looked at her husband, bit her lip, and stopped talking. She took my hand in hers, and I turned back to the window to watch the scenery pass.

✵

As we drove through Berlin, it seemed as if we were in a different world. People were outside, talking with one another, smiling and laughing as if everything was fine and I was not in a car with two complete strangers. Some of the buildings we passed had been damaged by bombs; those that had not stood proudly, old spires gleaming high into the sky.

It seemed as if pictures and posters of Hitler covered every building and house of the city. His cold, hard eyes looked down, assuring us that Germany reigned supreme.

Milada, Milada, Milada. As we drove, my fingers found the outline of Grandmother's star pin under my skirt.

We continued beyond Berlin, then north to the small town of Fürstenberg and into what looked like a woods. At last the trees gave way to a small clearing, and the car slowed as we turned into a long paved driveway that ended at the top of a hill. There was a sharp, unpleasant smell in the air that began to creep into the car.

A large white house stood before us, resting like a giant island in a sea of green grass. It was three stories tall, with dozens of windows and huge pillars that supported a large porch that wrapped around the house. I was awed and overwhelmed by its size. I had never seen a house so large.

We had come to the Werner residence.

The smell I had noticed at the foot of the driveway grew stronger as we approached the house, and I put a hand to my nose. It was a bitter smell, hanging in the air like a ghost—invisible yet present.

"Don't worry, liebling, you'll get used to the smell." Frau Werner patted my hand. "It's really not so bad," she said with a sigh. "Just the cost of war."

The chauffeur parked at the top of the circular driveway, then got out and opened the doors for us.

"Vater!" A child's high-pitched, delighted scream bounced toward us as we walked to the main entrance of the house. A young boy with short, silky blond hair and emerald-green eyes darted from the front door and jumped straight into Herr Werner's arms.

"Peter!" Herr Werner smiled, twirling his son around like an airplane.

A pretty young girl with bobbed blond hair and dark-blue eyes stood on the porch, smiling shyly. Frau Werner led me to her.

"Elsbeth, this is your new sister, Eva."

The girl smiled at me and touched my arm. "Hello, Eva," she said. I gazed at her in return, saying nothing, then let her take my hand and lead me into the house.

I slept in a real bed that night for the first time since I could remember. I wore a new nightdress that had pretty lace trim on its short sleeves, and I lay wrapped in cool, clean sheets. Like Elsbeth and Peter, I had my own bedroom as well as a separate room for a study. The walls in my room were painted pink, with matching lace curtains that puffed gently from the spring breeze coming through the window. It brought with it the sharp smell I had noticed earlier.

"Eva?" Frau Werner stood in the bedroom doorway, her body framed by the light from the hall. I was filled with aching and loneliness. I could not remember any other time when I had wanted my own mama more than at that moment.

"Yes?" I answered, sitting up. My voice sounded strange, almost as if it was coming from someone else. My own mama and papa had not come for me. I was to be Eva, German girl. I was to live with these people and call them Mother and Father and Sister and Brother. I was the new hope for Germany.

Frau Werner sat on my bed and began to stroke my hair and my face. Her hand was soft, her nails shortly trimmed. She started humming, and tears began to fall down my face.

"Shh, Eva, liebling. Shh." She pulled me onto her lap, whispering and rocking me gently. I let her hold me, feeling ashamed. She was a Nazi. She was the enemy. She had invaded my land and taken me from my home. And yet she was a woman, my new mother, there to comfort and hold me. I couldn't help but feel safe and protected in her arms.

Her golden hair was pulled out of its bun and hung long and loose, curling around her arms, brushing my shoulders. It was soft and smelled like flowers, and I ran my fingers through it, pulling apart small strands so they could catch the light from the hall.

"Your hair. It's beautiful," I whispered. She smiled, pulling me from her so she could see my face.

"You have beautiful hair too, Eva. Perfect German hair."

I winced. Nazi hair. Hair that my real mother and grandmother used to brush and braid and weave flowers into.

"We can style your hair," she continued. "Tomorrow if you wish. Oh, Eva, Elsbeth and I have so many things to share. She has been so excited to have a sister. And I to have another daughter."

She stood suddenly, brushing a tear off her cheek. "You must sleep now, precious Eva." She leaned over and kissed me on the forehead. Then, turning away, she walked out to the hall, her flowery scent staying behind with me, masking the strong smell coming from outside.

I lay in the dark, tracing Grandmother's pin beneath my nightdress and picturing the faces of Jaro and Anechka, Mama and Papa. A shadowy question was lurking in my mind. I no longer wondered when my family would come for me. For the first time, I began to wonder *if* they would come for me.

Where could they be?

Were they back home in the house I had grown up in, tucked safely into their own beds? Were they in a work camp, waiting to be freed so they could come rescue me? Were they living somewhere else in the world that I didn't even know about? Were they safe? Happy? Did they know I had become a German girl, the enemy? Were they thinking of me or had I been forgotten?

Milada, Milada, Milada.

I could almost hear the name on the breeze blowing in through the window and filling the lace curtains.

eight

May 1944: Fürstenberg, Germany

THE next morning I was awakened by happy shouts coming from Peter's study.

I slipped out of bed and crept down the hall, following the noise to the doorway. I stood there watching Peter and his father wrestle playfully on the floor.

"Vater! Vater! I will get you, Vater!" Peter pounced on top of Herr Werner, who sat crouched on the floor like a cat, with his shirt untucked and his uniform jacket slung over a chair.

"Ah! What a man you are!" Herr Werner growled playfully and rolled Peter onto his back, tickling him. "What a big strong man you are!" Peter was still dressed in his sleeping clothes, his hair sticking out in all directions.

"Hans," Frau Werner was standing behind me.

Peter and Herr Werner both stopped in mid-play,

and Herr Werner frowned at his wife. Peter looked from his mother to his father and then at me.

"Play is good for the boy. Helps him to be a man." Herr Werner ran his fingers through his son's hair. Peter giggled.

"Hans," Frau Werner repeated, her voice tight. "It is time for his bath."

"I'll send him when we're done, wife." He didn't look at her as he spoke but winked at Peter, cuffing him playfully on the shoulder.

"Come, Eva, it is time for your bath as well." Frau Werner turned briskly.

Peter followed his mother with his eyes, and when she was no longer in sight, he looked up at me and stuck out his tongue. I blinked in surprise. I had not been around boys for some time, but it reminded me of something my own brother would have done. Then I followed his mother to the washroom that Elsbeth and I were to share. It was large and gleaming white, with two separate claw-foot tubs. One was already full of water and bubbles.

"Our maid, Helga, drew the water for you," Frau Werner said as she led me into the room. "Here is a robe. The towels there are yours." She pointed to two soft white towels hanging from a gold loop by the tub and left me to my bath. Her manner had changed from the previous night. She had become brisk and efficient, a mother getting her daughter ready for the day.

I climbed into the tub and sat, breathing in the

scent of lavender and letting the warmth seep its way into my skin. I lifted small handfuls of water and watched it drip between my fingers. From down the hall came the sounds of Herr Werner leading Peter, finally, to a bath in his own washroom.

The water felt soft and luxurious. I couldn't remember the last time I had taken a bath. We had taken quick, cold showers at the center and had scrubbed with soap that always smelled like medicine. The showers left me feeling awake, but never feeling good or even really clean.

After my bath I ate breakfast by myself in the kitchen and was happy to be left alone. I could hear the sounds of Peter and Elsbeth getting ready for the day and their mother trying to hurry them along. The voices of servants echoed from various parts of the house, and periodically I would hear Herr Werner's loud voice or heavy footsteps upstairs. I sat eating quietly, wondering what was to happen to me in this house with this family.

※

I was left to myself for much of my first couple of days in the Werner household, and I spent that time trying to find my way around the inside of the huge house and wading through the great sea of lawn outside.

I was away from guards for the first time in two years, and I thought about running away. I could have escaped into the small woods that bordered the house, running until I couldn't run anymore and then lying down to sleep in the hope of awakening from this nightmare, back in my bed in Lidice. But each time I thought about leaving, something stopped me.

It was the smell that clung to everything inside and outside of the house. It was unlike anything I had smelled before, and it seemed to be everywhere at once, but its cause remained unseen. Some days it was strong, almost overpowering, while other days it was barely present. I knew something nearby had to be causing it, something unknown and awful. It was the fear of what I might find that kept me from running.

Elsbeth sometimes followed those first few days, hovering behind me. She obviously wanted to be near but was trying to stay far enough away to give me some privacy. She would keep a watchful eye over me until her mother or one of the servants shooed her away or assigned her an errand or chore.

As I wandered through the house, I was struck by how much it reminded me of a museum I had visited once in Prague, with its ornate artwork and dark wood paneling. Everything in the house was lavish and splendid, so perfect that I was afraid I might break something if I touched it.

Besides the bedrooms and studies, there was a huge sunroom on the second floor, which opened onto a large porch that wrapped all the way around the second story of the house. Peter's dog, Kaiser, would sit on the back porch with me and chase the butterflies that came to rest on the flowers. Helga, the maid, made sure there were always fresh flowers in the house, as if trying to use their fragrance to mask the ever-present smell.

A huge formal ballroom took up most of the first floor. One side opened onto a wide spiral staircase that elegantly swept up to the second floor. On the center wall of the ballroom was a framed picture of Hitler. It was almost life size and was accompanied by two red flickering candles and a vase of fresh flowers.

Next to the staircase was a library, with shelf after shelf of books that reached all the way to the ceiling. Some shelves were so high that a special ladder with wheels was needed to reach the books. In all my life I had never seen so many books.

Across from the library was the only room in the Werner house that was locked. Its door was plain compared with everything else in the house, and when I first found it, I thought perhaps it led to a washroom or closet. I turned the knob, but it refused to open. I shook the handle gently, and suddenly Peter was standing between the door and me.

"You can't go in there." His green eyes pierced me from beneath his short blond bangs.

"I—I didn't know," I stammered, pulling my hand away. I hadn't even been aware that he was following me.

"It's Vater's office, and he is the only one allowed inside. Sometimes I can go in. But you cannot." His eyes flashed with an adult kind of authority and narrowed to slits. Suddenly, I felt afraid.

"All right," I told him. "I didn't know."

"You will get in trouble if you ever go in there."

"I understand, Peter. I understand," I said, smiling at him uneasily. He crossed his arms and planted his feet in a firm stance.

"Vater is a very important man, you know. Very important," he said.

Elsbeth appeared next to Peter, nudging him aside. "Come now, Peter. Leave Eva alone. Cook made some treats for you."

"Chocolate biscuits?" Peter's face broke into a grin, and he uncrossed his arms, looking like a little boy again.

"Of course! Hurry, while they are still warm."

We watched him run off to the kitchen, then Elsbeth turned to me, her face serious. "Peter's right. About both things."

"What things?"

"Vater has an important job in the Nazi party, and you will get in trouble if you go in there. It's his office and he keeps it locked. Not even Mutter is allowed in. Peter is allowed sometimes, but no one else. You must stay away." Her eyes locked on mine, and something in her voice told me I shouldn't ask any more questions.

Herr Werner both frightened and fascinated me. His eyes were like Fräulein Krüger's, pleasant on the outside but hiding something hateful and frightening inside. He was tall and muscular but had a round belly that protruded over his belt. His mustache was always perfectly trimmed, and yet his hair flew wildly about his face, as if he often ran his fingers through it. He wore a lot of cologne, but that never quite covered the other smells that constantly clung to him: cigar smoke, wine, and that same smell that hung in the air around the house.

I had been instructed to call him Vater, but I tried not to call him by that if I could. I could hardly get the word out of my mouth without choking.

He was nothing like my own papa, who was short and trim with dark, gentle eyes that folded into small wrinkles at the corners when he laughed. There was nothing mysterious or hidden about my papa. He was who he was: strict but fair and kind to everyone. And someday, I knew, my own papa would come for me.

Herr Werner seemed to have only a certain amount of kindness within him, as if it was something that would run dry if he used too much of it. He was rough and rude with his servants and barely tolerated Elsbeth and her mother. But with Peter he was always kind and gentle, showing a side of himself I would not have believed existed if I had not seen him playing with his son. Because of this, I did not trust him.

After two days of watching me wander through the house, Elsbeth grew tired of following. She became my guide, leading me through various rooms and telling me stories that went with each.

"This is our recreation room," she said, leading me down a staircase near the kitchen and into a huge finished basement. It was fully equipped with games, exercise weights, a phonograph, and a dartboard. One side had a huge floor-length mirror and another side had a ballet barre attached to the wall.

I nodded, not saying anything, letting her lead the way. Like every other part of the house, the basement was large and elegant, although it was cool and smelled musty. At one end was a hall that led to a room, about the size of the formal dining room, and an even smaller room off of that. Elsbeth stopped at the entrance to the first room.

"This," her voice became a whisper, "is for air raids."

I nodded. Even though the Nazis had been in Czechoslovakia for three years before I left, I had not experienced air raids until I was at the center. The raids had been frightening, horrible things that happened during the night. A shrill whistle from the guard awakened us, and we would spring into well-rehearsed action, covering the windows with blankets and huddling together in a lower-level room. There we would stay, listening to the windows upstairs rattle and shake as planes carrying bombs droned close overhead. Even though we always emerged safe, I never slept well for many nights afterward.

I had heard no such sounds since arriving at the Werner house.

"We are far enough away from the fighting," Elsbeth said, shaking me out of my thoughts. "But Vater is very important, you know, and we live very close to his work. He is the commandant of a prison camp." She looked at me and patted my arm. "But don't worry," she added, suddenly cheerful again. "We have never needed this place.

"And this," Elsbeth continued, "is a most special radio. It uses batteries and can be taken anywhere. Mutter has another one upstairs in her sewing room just like this one. She likes to stay informed as to how the war is progressing."

There was a war. It could be easy to forget that while living in this place, in the midst of such luxury and quiet. Were there really people still fighting against the Nazis? By now I was sure they must be in charge of the whole world.

I nodded again, following Elsbeth back upstairs. Besides their maid, Helga, and their butler, Erich, the Werners had the chauffeur, Johann, a groundskeeper, Karl, and a cook, Inge, all of whom lived in a smaller house close to the edge of the woods. Inge was old and wrinkly and very fat. The Werners never called her by her real name but referred to her simply as Cook, a name she seemed to embrace. She made the most delicious foods I had ever eaten. Her meals were rich and filling and mixed with spices and textures I had not tasted before.

Usually we children and Mutter ate in a small dining room off the kitchen. If Herr Werner came home from work early enough, the entire family would eat together in the formal dining room, which had a long dark wood table and a huge chandelier hanging above it. The crystals of the chandelier twinkled and glittered with light from the small candles hidden inside its dozens of crystal cups. Before dinner Helga would climb a ladder and light each candle individually. Even though there was an electric light nearby, the Werners were very proud of this antique chandelier.

My first dinner in the formal dining room took place on my third night in the Werner house. Cook served plates and plates of delicious foods: bratwurst, Wiener schnitzel, sauerkraut, and strudel.

"Did you enjoy your dinner, Eva?" Mutter asked as we finished dessert.

"Delicious, thank you." My voice sounded strange to me when I spoke, echoing in the large space of the dining room.

"We have only the best," Herr Werner replied, finishing the wine in his glass in one gulp.

I ate the last bite of my strudel and stood, taking my dish off the table and reaching for Elsbeth's at my side. An immediate and absolute silence filled the room, and everyone froze in place. Peter's eyes widened and he stared at me, his spoon in midair. I quickly put the plates back on the table and sat down, realizing I had done something wrong. My cheeks burned with embarrassment.

"Eva." Mutter's voice was firm. "The servants are here to clear the table. It is not proper for you to do this chore."

Everyone remained still, and the room stayed

unearthly quiet. I braced myself for what was to come from Herr Werner, sure that beatings were within his nature.

Helga suddenly rushed in to clear the table, and her quick movement so startled me that I did what I had done repeatedly at the center.

"Heil Hitler!" I said, giving the Nazi salute toward the picture of Hitler on the wall. "I apologize to the Führer and to the family."

Mutter released a small sigh, and Herr Werner nodded at me and then at Helga.

Everyone relaxed while Helga finished taking the dishes away. I sat with my hands in my lap, looking down at the now-empty table.

For the rest of that evening and late into the night, something restless and ugly swirled inside me. I was bothered, but I wasn't sure by what. I tried to tell myself that it was because I wasn't used to having people serve me. But deep down I knew that wasn't really what had upset me.

My mind kept replaying the scene from dinner. I had made a mistake, and I had apologized by making the Nazi salute. It wasn't as if I had never made the salute before—I had made it every morning for two years at the center. What bothered me was how naturally it had come to me earlier that night—almost as if it was something I had grown up doing.

✳

A few days later Peter came dashing into the sunroom, dropped a letter in my lap, and ran back out.

My hands began to shake as I opened it and realized it was from Franziska.

6 May 1944

Dearest Eva,

This letter brings you many good wishes. I have been adopted by the loveliest of families in Berlin. I understand you are living very close to us in Fürstenberg—only an hour by car, even less by train. You must come visit soon! I am also to understand that your father is a high-ranking Nazi. How lucky for you! My father is a Nazi soldier who works at the processing center here in Berlin. I have two younger twin sisters who are quite adorable. They keep Mutter and me very busy. I have also made two new friends, Hilde and Berta. We attend the school that is near our house. I have even become friends with a boy, Kellen, who shares many of my interests. Please write soon, Eva, and tell me all about your family. I look forward to receiving your letter.

Yours truly,
Franziska Schönfelder

I sat and stared at the letter for a long time. Franziska Schönfelder. Ruzha had faded to a distant echo: a shadow, no longer even so much as a name. I stood and paced the room, my stomach churning. Snatches of a conversation I had had with Franziska at the center replayed in my head.

"My family is dead," Franziska had said. "They were killed in an Allied air raid."

I looked down at the piece of paper and noticed that my hands were still trembling. Angrily, I ripped the letter into little pieces and threw it into the empty fireplace. Ruzha was gone forever, replaced by a German girl named Franziska.

✳

As I adjusted to life with the Werners, I settled into the family's routine. Peter boarded the bus to attend school in Fürstenberg each morning, while Elsbeth and I stayed home for our training. We started with early-morning calisthenics, to keep our bodies healthy, and then turned to home economics lessons. In the afternoon we studied math or science, but we never went beyond simple addition and subtraction or the biology of children and race. Mutter had her teaching degree and provided all our lessons. But I found myself missing the kind of school we'd had at the center, with teachers and students and breaks for lunch. Mutter and Elsbeth were helpful and patient, but everything was the same, day after day, and boredom quickly set in.

One afternoon Mutter decided we needed to

practice polishing silver so we would know how to prepare for entertaining important guests. The three of us were in the formal dining room near the large china cabinet where the silver was stored. Mutter reached into a drawer and took out a small jar of black polish. Its round shape and metal top brought back a memory of a similar jar I had once held in my hand. A jar of homemade hair straightener for Terezie.

I had always loved Terezie's hair, even though she had not. She had inherited the dark-brown curls of her aunt and despised the way they refused to be tamed. I would try to braid her hair, but it wouldn't stay in the braids for longer than a few hours. Then little puffs of hair would rebel and start escaping.

So one day we had tried using a hair-straightening remedy of my grandmother's. It consisted of a variety of foul-smelling kitchen ingredients, including vinegar and raw eggs, which we mixed together and put into a small jar that looked like the silver-polish jar. Terezie and Grandmother and I had spent an entire Saturday afternoon wrapping Terezie's hair in corn husks that we had soaked in the awful-smelling solution.

But after being released from the husks, Terezie's hair was even wilder than usual, and she didn't speak to me for a whole week after that. I tried everything I could think of to get her to forgive me, even passing notes of apology to her during class—a risky venture under our teacher's watchful eye. Terezie had finally responded to one of my notes in her perfect swirly handwriting. *Dear Eva,* she had written.

I shook my head. No, she hadn't written that name. She had written a different name.

"Eva."

I jumped and looked around, remembering that I was in the Werner dining room.

"Eva!" It was Elsbeth. She was shaking me.

"Eva, are you well?" Mutter, still holding the small jar of polish, came over and put her hand on my forehead.

"Yes. I . . . I was just thinking." I looked at the jar in Mutter's hands.

"Well, you need to begin polishing," she said briskly, handing the polish to Elsbeth. "Peter will be home soon."

Mutter left the room, and I picked up a silver candlestick.

"Eva, oh, Eva . . . ," Elsbeth called out in a sing-song voice.

I turned to see that she had dabbed a small amount of black polish under her nose and chin to make it look as if she had a mustache and goatee. "Heil Hitler!" she said in a deep voice, and we both started giggling. Her antics kept me laughing and made the polishing go quickly.

Elsbeth was funny and smart and easy to like. I began to look forward each night to the time after dinner, when we would go to her room to knit or look through movie magazines. Sometimes we would talk about movie stars—which ones we thought were the most beautiful or whose clothes we liked best. Other times we would just sit quietly, letting the room fill with the soft clicking of our knitting needles.

One evening, when Elsbeth and I were in her room knitting scarves, the sound of laughter from the yard below brought us both to her window. Herr Werner was home early from work. He and Peter were in the yard, playing tag on the grass. Herr Werner was laughing, a deep belly laugh that boomed across the yard. We watched them play for a while, then went back to sitting on the bed. Elsbeth sighed.

"He likes Peter best, you know." Her tone was flat.

"What?" I asked, surprised by the certainty in her voice.

"He likes Peter best. He told me once. He thinks Peter will grow to be a fine German Nazi, ready to build the new Germany for Hitler. But me . . ."

I touched her shoulder. "I'm sure it's not that way. He's just busy or—"

"No," she said, looking past me toward the window. "It *is* that way. It will always be that way." She shook her head and forced a smile. "Let me show you the next stitch," she said, picking up her needles. Her hair fell in short waves above her shoulders, and her fingers worked with the yarn swiftly, her needles clacking lightly together and apart, together and apart.

Peter was a complicated part of Elsbeth's life. He knew he was the favored child, and he used his father's adoration to get his way at everyone else's expense. Sometimes Elsbeth appeared to only tolerate Peter. Other times she seemed to genuinely care about him and have true affection for him.

One afternoon Peter arrived home from school in a particularly grumpy mood. Unable to find anything to do, he began following Elsbeth and me, copying everything we said and did.

"Come on, Eva, let's go outside and sit on the grass," Elsbeth said.

"Come on, Eva," Peter copied, using a false, high-pitched voice, "let's go outside and sit on the grass."

"Just ignore him, Eva. He's an ill-mannered child," said Elsbeth.

"Just ignore him, Eva," Peter continued. "He's an ill-mannered child."

We walked out to the lawn in the back of the house. The smell was strong that day, but we ignored it, as we always did, and made our way to the edge of the grass where the woods began. Peter followed, walking as if he was wearing high heels. Kaiser trailed Peter, sniffing the ground and wagging his tail madly.

Elsbeth and I walked a few more yards. Then she turned suddenly and charged at her brother. Peter screamed in fright and took off running for the house with Kaiser close at his heels. But Elsbeth was too quick. She easily grabbed Peter and wrestled him to the ground, tickling him until he was giggling helplessly.

"Stop, Elsbeth! Stop! Please!" he begged.

"Are you going to stop following Eva and me?" Elsbeth had him pinned to the ground with her knees.

"Yes! Yes!" Peter choked out between giggles.

"And do you admit that I am your queen and you are my slave?" Elsbeth demanded.

"No! You're nothing but a stupid girl!" Peter spit out, still giggling.

"Say it!" Elsbeth pulled off one of his shoes and socks and started tickling his toes. I stood off to the side by myself but smiled, thinking of the times Jaro and I had fought like that.

"All right, all right. You are my queen and I am your slave," Peter muttered.

"Louder!"

"You are my queen and I am your slave!" Peter screamed, the sound reverberating through the trees at the edge of the woods. Elsbeth let go of his arms, and he lay on the grass, panting, while Kaiser licked his face. Suddenly, Peter sat up and reached for Elsbeth, trying to tickle her. But she was too big for him, and he couldn't get her down.

"Oh, Peter. Your nose," Elsbeth said. A small trickle of blood had begun to run from Peter's nose. "I'm sorry." She took a handkerchief from her skirt and began dabbing it above his lip.

"No, like this," I said, hurrying over to them. I

squeezed the handkerchief on the bridge of Peter's nose, as I had learned in my first-aid lessons at the center.

"It's not bad," Peter said, looking from Elsbeth to me. "I won't tell Vater."

Elsbeth helped Peter up and slowly walked with him back to the house. I hung back, watching, and realized that I had come to genuinely care for them both.

✳

Just as I enjoyed spending the evenings with Elsbeth, I also began to look forward to bedtime each night, when Mutter would come to my room to tuck me in. I loved the feel of her hands playing with my hair and the smell of flowers that always floated around her.

One night, several weeks after my arrival, she stayed longer than usual, running her fingers through my hair and humming softly. I was almost asleep when she spoke.

"Eva?"

"Yes?" I opened my eyes.

"What kind of cake is your favorite?"

"Cake?" I asked, confused.

"Well, we were going to surprise you, but . . ." Her voice was quick and sounded nervous. "There is going to be a party. In your honor. And I want Cook to make your favorite cake. It's an adoption party. For you. In your honor." Her words spilled out, stumbling over one another and repeating.

I could no longer feel her hands. It was as if my whole body had gone numb.

"Your vater wanted it to be a surprise, but I felt you should know so you can help plan the party. He gave me permission to tell you and—"

"I am being adopted," I said, cutting her off in mid sentence.

"Yes, Eva." She stopped talking and looked at me.

I got out of bed and walked to the window, feeling the wooden floor beneath my bare feet. I stared into the darkness for several seconds, steadying myself against the rush of hopelessness washing over me.

I swallowed hard. Mutter continued talking.

"It's going to be so lovely. Cook was planning on a chocolate cake because Elsbeth thought that might be your favorite." She came over and touched my shoulder. "There will be decorations and pretty clothes and a special ceremony."

"But . . . ," I began, trying to hold back the tears.

"I knew you would be happy," Mutter continued, oblivious to me. "You must come now and get back into bed." She led me to my bed and pulled the sheet over me. "You need lots of rest, my Eva. The party is only three weeks away, and there's so much to do." She leaned over and kissed me, then turned out the light and left.

I lay in bed, unable to move. It was final. Hope was gone. Mama and Papa were not coming for me. I was never going home.

When I finally fell asleep hours later, I dreamed of my grandmother. She sat in a small room that seemed strange and yet familiar. My bedroom in Lidice. I reached for my grandmother and tried to call her, but my voice made no sound.

When I opened my eyes, I was in a room painted pink, with matching lace curtains and a large picture of Hitler on the wall. Early light was just beginning to creep through the windows. From someplace far off, a mourning dove called to signal the dawn. The whole world should awake, the dove seemed to cry. Something new is beginning.

nine

June 1944: Fürstenberg, Germany

A few days later Mutter called me into her sewing room. I walked in to find Elsbeth already standing there.

"Eva," Mutter said, holding up a stunning long blue dress. "This is for you."

"It's beautiful," I whispered, reaching out to touch the soft fabric.

"Mutter made it for you," Elsbeth said, smiling.

"It's for your adoption party," Mutter added. I looked into her eyes. Even though she was smiling, I could tell she was nervous. This person wanted me and loved me and somehow even needed me. I felt a lump in my throat. "Do you like it?" she asked.

"It's beautiful," I repeated, awed that someone would make something so lovely for me.

"Why don't you try it on, liebling?" Mutter said softly, handing the dress to me.

I took it to my room and held it in front of me as I looked at myself in the mirror. It was made of soft blue satin that matched the color of my eyes almost perfectly.

I pulled my skirt off and laid it on my bed, reaching inside by habit to remove Grandmother's pin. I ran my fingers over the pin, then touched the soft material of the dress. I was afraid the pin might tear the delicate fabric, so I pulled a soft lace handkerchief from the top drawer of my dresser. Carefully, I wrapped the little pin inside, then placed it gently back in the drawer, where it would be safe.

Then I slipped on the dress and twirled a few times in front of the mirror. It fit perfectly.

Mutter appeared in the doorway. "It fits," she said, with tears in her eyes. "I'm so glad."

"A party will be fun, yes?" Elsbeth asked, standing next to her.

I nodded yes, twirling again before the mirror and wondering if this was how a princess feels.

✢

The house hummed with the energy of party preparations during the next three weeks. Mutter was sewing red satin banners to hang in the ballroom, and Cook was busy experimenting with recipes for the menu. Herr Werner had come home from work early several days in a row to help with preparations, and even Peter seemed less pesky than usual.

Elsbeth and I were assigned to embroider small patterns on the table linens. One evening we were sitting together in my room working on our task with the windows open. The breeze outside rustled gently through the trees, and the smell was barely present that night. Everything felt right at that moment, as if I really did belong to a family again.

As we sewed, I had a sudden clear thought of my grandmother and the way she would sit in her rocking chair and tat, using a small silver shuttle to create delicate lace handkerchiefs and table coverings.

"This is like . . ." I suddenly wanted to tell Elsbeth about the silver shuttle and tatting and my grandmother. I wanted to tell her everything about my family, while the memory was so clear and beautiful. But it was as if a black cloud had come to rest over part of my brain. I couldn't remember the name I used to call my grandmother in the language I had grown up speaking.

"Like what?" Elsbeth put down her thread, turning to face me.

"Like . . ." I started again. "I don't remember." I stood and paced, trying to pinpoint the exact moment when that precious word had slipped out of my mind. How had that happened?

"Well, if you don't remember, it can't be that important." Elsbeth turned back to her embroidery, frowning over a stitch.

I lay in bed late into the night, searching once again for the Czech name I had called my grandmother.

But I couldn't find it.

I searched for other Czech names, other phrases, and realized I could no longer remember the words I had grown up speaking. Tears rolled down my cheeks as I discovered that another part of myself had slipped from my grasp, like a balloon floating quietly into the sky. And I hadn't even seen it leave.

✳

A few evenings later Elsbeth and I were eating dinner with Mutter. Herr Werner was working late, and Peter was at a friend's house. We were sitting at the small table in the informal dining room finishing our meal when Cook came in with a mixing bowl and two spoons.

"I am perfecting the cake batter for the party. Would you young women wish to lick the bowl?" she asked with a twinkle in her eyes, knowing what the answer would be.

"Absolutely!" Elsbeth replied, jumping up and reaching for the bowl.

"Wait, Elsbeth. I don't want you making a mess in the house. Go outside," Mutter said.

I took the spoons, and Elsbeth led the way to the porch. Kaiser followed, wagging his tail wildly to let us know he wanted in on the treat. The batter was rich and creamy, and we cleaned the bowl with our spoons, letting Kaiser take a little from our fingers. Then we lay down looking up at the night sky. The back porch was perfect for stargazing.

Thousands of stars gleamed and twinkled in the

summer evening. Elsbeth and I lay a long time without speaking as Kaiser settled between us.

"I wonder why the stars blink like that," Elsbeth said, breaking the silence. "They look like little candles in the sky."

"I'm not sure." I answered. "I know each star is like the sun. They're huge and full of heat and light and gas."

"It's too bad the smell is so strong tonight. I could look at the stars for hours," Elsbeth said after several minutes.

"Yes. I'm starting to get a headache from it. I think we should go in," I said.

"The smokestacks must be working hard," she said, sitting up.

"Smokestacks?" I asked. "Is it smokestacks that make the smell?" I had never heard anyone talk about what caused it. "Where are they?"

"They're at the camp where Vater is commandant," Elsbeth answered.

"I thought he worked at a prison camp," I said.

"He does."

"So why are there smokestacks there? What do they have to burn if it's a prison camp?" I asked.

"They don't burn things you'd normally burn in them, Eva. I heard Vater talking to Mutter one day." I could tell Elsbeth was trying to say something but was having trouble.

"I don't understand," I said.

"Eva." Elsbeth's voice softened. "There is much

sickness in the camp. Prisoners, well, prisoners die. And there isn't room to bury them. So the smoke-stacks—"

"Oh." I held up a hand to stop her from saying more. "Oh," I repeated, as my stomach started to hurt more than my head. "I don't want to talk about it anymore," I said.

Elsbeth nodded and stood, gathering the bowl and spoons before walking back into the house. Despite the smell, I stood a while longer on the porch before following her inside. I looked up at the stars blinking in the darkness, wishing I hadn't asked about the smokestacks and wishing I didn't know the cause of the smell.

ten

On the day of my adoption party, the house over-
flowed with people. Dozens of Nazis in highly decorated uniforms stood arm in arm with beautifully
dressed women. The entire house shimmered with
noise and laughter and happiness.

Outside, shiny black cars lined the driveway.
Chauffeurs gathered in a large, festive tent set up on
the lawn, smoking, drinking beer, and laughing.

I walked through the rooms downstairs, awed by
the beauty and pageantry, amazed that it was all for
me. My stomach was jittery with both nervousness
and excitement. I felt like a princess in my beautiful
long blue gown, and pinned at the top was a fresh red
rose corsage. Mutter had styled my hair, wrapping it
on top of my head in a graceful swirl that was framed
by tiny white flowers. I stood for a moment in front
of the mirror in the downstairs hallway, admiring

my hair and the soft fabric of my dress. I was still amazed by the way the blue of the gown matched the blue in my eyes.

A young man and woman stood at the bottom of the winding staircase in the front entry room. I walked by the couple on my way up the stairs just as Erich was handing them glasses of punch. Seeing me, the woman gasped in delight and pulled me to her.

"Eva! Come, dear! Here, Gerald. Raise your glass to Eva and to the new Germany!"

"Heil Hitler!" The young man raised his glass and winked at me. I nodded, smiling, and continued up the staircase.

Children raced everywhere upstairs, giggling and screaming.

"Eva!" Elsbeth squealed as I passed her doorway. She was sitting with two other girls but jumped up to grab my hand and pull me into the room. She wore a long white gown that Mutter had made, with a League of German Girls sash draped across the front and pinned at the top with a white rose corsage.

"Come meet my friends." She led me over to where the other girls stood. "Lotte, Willa, this is Eva. My . . . sister." It was the first time she had called me her sister, and she smiled at me as she said it.

"Eva, it is so nice to meet you!" Lotte came over and put an arm around my shoulder.

"Yes. I wish I had a sister," Willa added.

Just then the tinny notes of a bugle filled the air, and the whole house grew quiet. Elsbeth looked at me. "Come, Eva. Downstairs."

The party guests made their way to the formal ballroom. There were so many people that they spilled into the front entry hall. Inside the ballroom the red satin banners that Mutter had sewn crisscrossed the ceiling from one side to the other. Vases and vases of red roses lined the walls, and dozens of small candles burned brightly beneath Hitler's picture.

Herr Werner and Mutter stood up on a small platform that had been placed at the front of the room. Peter stood next to them, a bugle in one hand. Mutter saw me and smiled, motioning for me to join her. Elsbeth gave me a gentle push. "Go on," she whispered. "This is for you."

Herr Werner smiled as I approached. It was a real smile, the first one I had ever seen him direct toward me. Feeling shy suddenly, I smiled back and moved closer to Mutter. Erich and Helga walked around the room quickly, filling everyone's glass with bubbling champagne.

"Friends and comrades," Herr Werner began. "Today we welcome our new German daughter, Eva, to our family. We are proud to now have three children to help build the new Germany."

Herr Werner looked at Mutter, whose eyes glistened with tears. She stepped down from the platform, and a man standing nearby lifted a small medal on a ribbon over her head and hung it around her neck.

"Heil Hitler!" Herr Werner barked, giving the Nazi salute.

"Heil Hitler!" we all repeated, loud enough to make the smallest crystals in the chandelier shimmer and send scattered light dancing across the faces. My arm went up with everyone else's in salute.

The man who had given the medal to Mutter stepped up to the platform. "And now a toast," he said, raising his glass. Everyone grew silent, even the children. "I make this toast to celebrate the Werner household for fulfilling their German duty by increasing their family's number to five. May they have many more successful adoptions!" He drank. Around us everyone toasted with their glasses, filling the house with the sounds of clinking crystal. "Heil Hitler!"

For the first time, I noticed that nearly all the women, except a young pregnant woman and a few others, wore medallions like the one Mutter had just received. Some of the medals were bronze, but most were silver.

"Now, honored guests and comrades," Herr Werner declared. "Cook has prepared a special meal in the dining room. Please, everyone, eat. Eat!" The guests murmured happily, moving toward the food. Elsbeth and her friends came to join me.

"Oh, Eva. Isn't this exciting?" Lotte clutched my hand in hers.

"Yes," I answered. "But what was that medal Mutter received? And the medals the other women are wearing?"

"My mutter has a medal," Lotte said.

"My mutter has a *gold* medal," Willa added.

Elsbeth rolled her eyes at Willa and snapped, "My mutter has only just started." Then she turned to me. "When a woman has at least three children, she is awarded the Mother's Cross, so everyone can see she is a good German citizen. Women who have four children wear the silver cross."

"And women with at least six children wear the gold one, like my mutter," Willa jumped in.

"Oh," I said, as I realized how much worth I had added to this family and feeling important somehow.

"Come, Eva. Let's eat!" Elsbeth said, pulling me toward the dining room and the huge mountain of food.

✳

Later, after the party had ended and the night had grown dark and cool and quiet, I sat alone on the porch swing at the back of the house, listening to the rhythmic creaking of the metal chain.

"Wasn't it nice today, Eva?" Elsbeth appeared and joined me on the swing, swaying in time to the rhythm I had started. She wore a pretty lace night-dress, and her hair was freshly washed, giving off the same light flower scent as her mother's.

"So nice," I answered, reaching over and squeezing her hand.

We sat and swung together awhile longer without talking. I looked up at the night sky dotted with stars, then back down at Elsbeth, and smiled. I felt content and full for the first time in a very long time.

eleven

October 1944: Fürstenberg, Germany

As the season changed from summer to autumn, other things began to change as well, both inside our house and in Germany itself.

Light frost began to cover the ground in the mornings, making everything look peaceful and pure. But the nights were filled with the sounds of war. Planes droned overhead, and on clear nights, if we stared long enough through the sunroom windows, Elsbeth and I could see the flash of bombs exploding in the distance. It was my first time seeing or hearing any of the fighting, and it made the house, which had always felt so big and safe, suddenly seem small and fragile.

Mutter began spending more time in her sewing room, listening to the radio she kept there. Lines of worry crept into her face, and she seemed distracted and edgy.

"It's the war," Elsbeth said one night when we were in her room knitting winter scarves. "I think"—she got up and closed the door—"I think our Führer . . ." She stopped and seemed unsure of how to continue. "I think our Germany is struggling," she whispered.

A wave of fear swept through me, and I put down my knitting needles. What did this mean?

"Vater would be angry to know this, but when Mutter listens to her radio in her sewing room, sometimes I listen, too, from the hall." She continued knitting, not looking at me. "The Allies have advanced."

"What does that mean?" I asked aloud, thoughts whirling in my head. Would I be taken away again? Adopted by someone new?

"Nothing, really." Elsbeth put her needles down and looked at me, forcing a smile. "I'm sorry, Eva. I shouldn't frighten you. You know how strong Germany is. We will prevail against our enemies. Everything will be fine."

Then she got up, and as she opened the door, Peter stumbled in. He had clearly been leaning against it, trying to hear our conversation. He dashed down the hall screeching, "Vater! Vater! Elsbeth and Eva had the door shut. They're telling secrets! Vater!"

Elsbeth rolled her eyes.

She held up the finished part of her scarf. "You know, Eva, perhaps I'll send this scarf to our soldiers fighting for Germany. It will help keep someone warm this winter. You should send yours, too."

I looked at my scarf, which was nearly complete. But no matter how hard I tried, I couldn't imagine it around the neck of a German soldier, helping to keep him warm.

※

The next day Mutter seemed preoccupied during our home economics lessons. "Perhaps it would be best if you girls went out for some exercise. Eva, you and Elsbeth pack a lunch and go for a walk. The cool autumn air will be good for you."

Elsbeth's eyes lit up. She had talked many times about wanting to show me the woods near the house. "Thank you, Mutter!" She jumped off her stool and went to the refrigerator.

"Thank you, Mutter," I repeated.

Mutter grabbed me in a hug. "Everything will be better when this war is over. Then we can forget what our enemies have done to us, and we will all rest easier." I nodded and went to get a blanket while Elsbeth packed lunch.

Once we had reached the woods, Elsbeth stopped, putting the picnic basket on the ground. It was a beautiful day, sunny and bright, and the air was cool and crisp, with only a trace of the smell.

"Ah, freedom!" Elsbeth took a deep breath, looking up at the sky and opening her arms to the sun. Suddenly, she tagged me. "You're it!" she screamed, then dashed off into the woods. Kaiser barked and ran after her.

We chased each other back and forth along a narrow path in the woods, with the sounds of fallen leaves crunching beneath our feet. Laughing and screaming, we ran until Elsbeth stopped and grew serious. I stood panting, listening to the sounds of birds chattering and the breeze rustling the brittle autumn leaves in the trees.

Elsbeth took my hand. "I have something to show you." She grinned mischievously.

"What?" I asked.

"It's a secret. You have to promise not to tell." She was whispering, and her eyes darted from side to side as if she was a spy checking for enemies.

"Of course," I promised.

She started skipping, making wide swoops around the woods. Kaiser followed, barking and leaping into the air. Laughing, I walked behind as Elsbeth left the path and made her way into a clearing. It was small, no bigger than our informal dining room. Three large oaks grew next to each other, a painted red bull's-eye resting in the middle of each trunk.

"Vater thinks I don't know. He thinks I am stupid. Well . . ." Elsbeth spread her arms and looked around the clearing.

"What? What is this?" I whispered, feeling a little frightened.

"This, my dear Eva"—she puffed out her chest and deepened her voice—"is where the men get to be men." She looked ridiculous strutting around the circle, her thin stomach extended to imitate her father's protruding belly. "I am Herr Werner, and this is my kingdom."

I laughed. It was a good imitation of her father.

She stopped, suddenly serious, and looked at me. "This is where Vater brings Peter to practice his shooting."

"Oh, a target range."

"And here," Elsbeth whispered, "is the best part." She walked behind one of the trees and tipped a boulder onto its side. In a shallow hole beneath it lay a small pistol and a large stock of ammunition.

"I have been doing my own practicing," Elsbeth said, her words quick with excitement. "I followed Peter and Vater here once and watched. They don't even know I have this. Here." She picked up the pistol and dropped it into my hand. "Have you ever shot a gun?"

I shook my head, even as I curled my fingers around the gun. It felt cool and light and was small enough to fit neatly into my palm, although the slender barrel stuck out far from my fingers. I remembered the times I had been at the other end of a gun, and a thrill of power swept through me. This time I was the one holding the weapon.

"Where did you get it?" I asked, turning the gun over in my hand.

"Vater accidentally left his office unlocked one day." Elsbeth spoke in a rush, her voice high and eager. "You should see what is there, Eva. Someday we will sneak in. There are official documents and maps and all sorts of things. And so many guns. He won't miss this little one. Let me show you how to load it." She took the gun and put bullets into its chamber.

Carefully Elsbeth showed me how to position my arm, where to look, and how to aim at the bull's-eye. In everything she did, Elsbeth was patient and a good teacher. She showed me how to shoot at the unmarked trees on the opposite side of the clearing so there wouldn't be any evidence that we had been there.

I caught on quickly. It took only a few tries before I could hit the trunks. By the time we finished, I was trembling with excitement. Elsbeth took the gun and shot several times. Her aim was perfect, and I could tell she was a natural marksman.

"Are you hungry?" she asked after her fifth shot.

"Starving," I said.

"I've got the perfect spot for a picnic."

We gathered the spent shells and the gun and safely tucked them into their hiding place beneath the boulder. Then we headed deeper into the woods.

Elsbeth's spot was nearly perfect. It was another small, secluded clearing with just enough room for a picnic. But the smell was stronger at this clearing than it had been at the other. I tried my best to ignore it as we laid the thick blanket on top of the fallen leaves and unpacked our lunch. Despite the smell, the sandwiches tasted hearty and fresh in the cool air. As we ate, Elsbeth gossiped about her friends.

"So then Lotte went right up and asked him to dance. Can you believe it?" Elsbeth exclaimed between bites. She was absorbed in a story about a Hitler Youth dance she had attended the year before with Lotte and Willa. Kaiser dozed on the ground near us. The exhilaration from learning to shoot was still with me.

"Really?" I asked.

"And then he said yes, and then they danced. I wish I could be so bold!"

I nodded. My experience with boys had been limited.

"I can't wait until this year's dance. We can go together, Eva, and maybe I will ask a boy to dance!"

"Maybe," I answered.

"It's getting late. We'd better go back. I don't think Vater would like it if he knew Mutter had allowed us an afternoon away from our lessons. We should be home before he arrives from work." We finished the rest of our picnic, and Elsbeth gathered up the blanket.

We stood and began walking back the way we had come. Elsbeth started humming the German national anthem. I hung back a bit and closed my eyes, lifting my face to the sun, not wanting our time in the woods to end. I let the warmth touch my cheeks and listened to Elsbeth's singing.

Suddenly, I heard a song coming from someone other than Elsbeth.

Where is my home? Where is my home?
Where brooks rumble through the meadow . . .

I opened my eyes again, not sure if I had really heard something or imagined it. The words were familiar and sweet, yet strange at the same time.

Elsbeth continued ahead of me, humming and putting her arm up in the Nazi salute. I squinted, trying to listen more carefully for what I had heard.

Pines murmur over the mountainside,
All the orchards are in bloom.

The words touched my ears a second time. They were the sounds of my Czech language! I stopped. Had I heard those words out loud? Elsbeth started imitating the Nazi march as more words came, this time even more clearly.

What an earthly paradise in view,
This is the beautiful land,
The land of Czechs, home of mine.

This time there was no mistake. Someone was singing in Czech, clear and beautiful. Singing just for me.

I started running—past Elsbeth, past Kaiser, past the trees and the war and the confusion, heading in the direction of those words.

The song grew louder and clearer as I stumbled

off the path and tore through the brush. Faster and faster I ran, getting closer and closer to the words, until suddenly I was stopped by a barbed-wire fence. I looked around, breathing heavily. I was at the edge of an immense clearing. The smell here was very strong, bitter and heavy. It was almost overpowering.

"Eva!" Elsbeth caught up with me and grasped my shoulder, out of breath from running. "Eva. What are you doing?"

About fifty feet away, on the other side of the barbed wire, women were breaking huge stones with large metal hammers and singing in time to their hammering.

Singing in Czech.

The language I'd thought I had lost forever shimmered, alive and real, in front of me. Even though I had forgotten the words, I could still recognize them as having once been mine.

And with its sounds came the realization that Mama and Papa could be here in this place right now. Waiting all this time for me to find them.

"I . . . ," I called out hoarsely to the women in German, my throat dry from running.

The women were horribly thin and hollow, with hair that was ragged and short. Each wore a striped dress marked with a red upside-down triangular patch. Inside the triangle was a large *T.* Hardly any of the women wore stockings, even though the autumn breeze was cool.

The women sang slowly, in time to their swings.

"I . . . ," I began again, unable to piece together what I wanted to say in Czech. I desperately needed to communicate, to discover how they had come to this place and to find out if Mama and Grandmother were with them or if the women knew anything of my village, my home.

"Eva!" Elsbeth turned me toward her.

"What is this place?" I gasped. "Who are these women?"

"This is Ravensbrück women's camp, Eva. This is the prison camp where Vater is commandant. These are his prisoners, very bad people. Many of them are Jews. We shouldn't be here. It is not allowed."

"No." I turned back toward the women and tried again to get my tongue to speak Czech, but no words would come. The women ignored me, continuing to strike the rocks at their feet.

I felt something breaking inside me, and I pounded my hands against the barbed-wire fence.

"Eva!" Elsbeth grabbed me and dragged me back into the forest.

"No!" I screamed again, feeling helpless and desperate and trying to reach for the women. Instead, I felt myself being pulled away from the beautiful sounds of the Czech words.

When Elsbeth finally let me go, we were back on the path in the woods. I looked at my hands and saw small lines of blood running down each palm like tiny rivers.

Elsbeth pulled a napkin from the picnic basket and dabbed at my hands. "You mustn't let Mutter see this, Eva. We will both be in trouble. Say nothing of this." Her voice was harsh and high-pitched. She pressed the napkin into my hand without looking at me and continued. "Do not ever come to this place again. You will get us both in trouble. It is a bad place, Eva. Do you understand? A very bad place."

We walked for a long time without talking. Questions and feelings tumbled around inside me. What exactly had I found, and what did it mean?

My hands were throbbing angrily but had stopped bleeding by the time we reached the backyard. Kaiser followed behind, whining softly, as if he sensed that something was not right. The breeze blew restlessly through the trees, carrying the camp, the song, and the women farther and farther away.

※

Inside the house I went straight to my room, unable to look at or speak to either Mutter or Elsbeth. I needed to be alone. As I passed Elsbeth's room, I noticed the scarf she had been knitting the night before. I stopped and looked at it. A scarf for a German soldier. While all this time my own people were cold, starving, and imprisoned in the woods behind the house.

In my own room I stood before the mirror and took in the reflection of the Aryan German girl staring back. I touched the blond hair and looked deep into the blue eyes, trying to see if there was any Czech girl left inside at all.

Who had I become? A German girl who gives the Hitler salute at dinner without thinking? I looked at my long plaid skirt, my well-fed body, and my rosy cheeks that were flushed from the warmth of the house.

How different from Franziska was I after all?

I stared for a moment longer as a dull ache spread through my stomach. Then I turned abruptly to get away from the mirror and the questions. I spent the rest of that day in a fog, knowing I had somehow found myself again but unsure what that truly meant.

✳

Strange images and words haunted my dreams that night, and I awoke suddenly, only a few hours after falling asleep. I sat up in bed, thinking about something real that I might have lost.

Grandmother's star pin.

How long had it been since I had touched or worn it? How could I have forgotten it? I pulled back the covers and crept out of bed. As quietly as I could, I opened the top drawer of my bureau and felt for the handkerchief. It was safe, exactly where I had left it months before. I hugged it tightly to my chest and got back into bed. With trembling hands I unwrapped the handkerchief. The pin was just as I remembered it. Gently I took it out and followed the outline of its star shape with my fingers. Then I touched each little garnet. Tears of relief came to my eyes as I reclaimed a tiny, but very real, part of my life.

I tried to picture Mama and Papa, my grandmother and Anechka, and my big brother, Jaro. How long had it been since I had thought of them? I pinned the little star into the folds of my nightdress so it would be next to me, and thought of the women in the camp. I traced the shape of their words in my mind, trying to whisper into the night in their language and trying to understand what the discovery of the camp meant.

twelve

As fall and then winter continued, the sky turned into a constant battleground. Plane engines droned, night and day, and were interrupted only by bursts of artillery fire. The tension outside had begun to seep inside the house as well, like a poisonous gas. It became clear that our resources were dwindling. The reality of war was creeping in.

Peter cried loudly when Mutter told Cook she would have to leave. "No, no!" he wailed, pulling at Cook's skirt. "She's my favorite, Mutter, my favorite!"

"Peter, this is how it must be," Mutter replied. But she too had tears in her eyes when she said good-bye.

Erich and Helga and the rest of the help were also let go. Mutter refused to give a reason when we asked why, but Elsbeth said it was because Herr

Werner could no longer afford to pay them. We were running low not only of money but of food as well. Sugar and flour and meat had become scarce. Peter often begged for more helpings at dinner, but there were none. My own stomach too had begun to rumble and complain with the soft gnaw of hunger.

"What about the food downstairs, the food that's stored in the shelter?" Elsbeth asked Mutter once, after another meal with little to eat.

"Nein!" Mutter snapped. "We don't need it. We are fine. Fine. No one is going hungry." She was spending all her time now hovering over Elsbeth and me, or sitting near the radio, working her needlepoint. Her eyes had grown puffy and tired looking.

Herr Werner stayed at work for days at a time. When he was home, he walked around frowning and mumbling to himself. His clothes were rumpled and dirty, and his mustache and beard went unshaved, growing ever wilder to match the crazed look that had come to rest in his eyes.

Elsbeth's and my lessons were forgotten, and we spent all our time together in either her bedroom or mine. Peter no longer attended school, and he stayed inside all day bothering us. No one, except Mutter and Herr Werner, was allowed to leave the house.

Things in Germany were changing.

I knew that things had changed within myself as well. I walked around aware of the war, and of the tension and fear in the house, but I was unsure what it all meant for me. Would I be taken away again?

Would Mama and Papa find me at last? Or were they truly gone, as Fräulein Krüger had said? Were the Werners my only family now? I thought often of the women in the camp, and as I lay in bed at night, tracing Grandmother's pin, I wondered what was going to happen to all of us.

✳

I awoke late one night to loud, angry sounds coming from Mutter and Herr Werner's room. Drawers banged open and shut. A glass broke. Harsh, angry words punctured the stillness of the house.

"Absolutely not! Hans! I don't know what you are thinking. Hans! Put your travel bag away."

"Trude, listen. The decision has been made. And not by me. I have no choice. What is important is—"

"What is important, Hans, is your family. You will leave us here alone? How will we know where you are? How will we know what to do? At least take us with you."

"You know that is not possible. Enough of this! You are acting foolish!"

"Hans!"

"Enough! I said enough!" There was the crack of a slap and then only the sound of banging drawers.

Quietly, I got out of bed and pulled my robe around my shoulders, then walked down the hall to Elsbeth's room. Peter was asleep in her bed, and she had her arm wrapped protectively around him. I could hear the sounds of bombs exploding in the distance.

"Did you hear them arguing?" I whispered. She nodded and motioned for me to sit on her bed.

"They are arguing about the war," she whispered back. "Vater has said Berlin may fall to the Americans and the Russians. They will be looking for all Nazis, especially important ones. Vater is afraid he will be arrested . . . or worse. That is what they are arguing about." She turned and looked down at Peter, gently smoothing his bangs away from his face. "Go back to bed, Eva. There is nothing you can do." I opened my mouth to say something, but she waved me away.

I tiptoed back to my room and got into bed, but I lay staring up at the ceiling. Only after many hours did I fall into a restless sleep.

The next morning I awoke to find the house quiet. Too quiet. There were no sounds of Peter or Elsbeth or anyone else moving about. I got out of bed and went downstairs, to find Mutter sitting near the kitchen window, sipping tea.

"Mutter?" I touched her arm.

She looked up at me and blinked. A red mark brightened one cheek.

"Mutter? Where is everyone?"

"Elsbeth is still sleeping, so be quiet, Eva. I don't want to wake her. Your vater has gone into hiding. The Russian troops are looking for Nazi officers. When it is safe, he will come for us. He promised."

"Peter?" My stomach lurched as I asked the question. "Where is Peter?"

"He and his dog are with your vater. They will come back for us." She grabbed my wrist, searching my eyes with hers. "He promised."

Elsbeth appeared in the doorway, still wearing her nightdress. Her eyes had dark circles under them, and her hair was uncombed and tangled.

"They are not coming back, Mutter," she said. "They are gone. And we need to leave too. It is not safe. Not safe at all."

"Nein." Mutter stood, knocking her teacup to the floor. "Nein!" She began pacing the floor of the kitchen, screaming. "This is my house. This is my family. We will not leave. Never! Hitler will keep us safe. We will wait until your vater returns for us. Heil Hitler!" She gave a weak Nazi salute.

Elsbeth turned and disappeared upstairs. I stood, unsure what to do and feeling completely helpless.

When Elsbeth came back, she carried the blankets and sheets from her bed. She dropped them into my arms. "Help me, Eva," she said briskly. Her tone with her mother was more gentle. "Sit down, Mutter. Have some tea." Mutter opened her mouth, then sat back down again, ignoring the broken cup that lay on the floor.

Elsbeth and I spent the rest of that day moving things into the shelter. It was much larger than I remembered from when Elsbeth had shown it to me shortly after my arrival. Tucked away in an earthen corner of the basement, the shelter actually had two rooms, one larger than the other, and a small washroom and toilet off to the side. In the smaller room was a mattress on a wooden platform that folded into the wall when it wasn't being used.

Between the two rooms was a pantry filled with canned fruits and vegetables, along with many sacks of dried meat and dried apples. There were even several dozen bottles of water all the way from Switzerland, in case our well became damaged or destroyed.

An entire wall in the larger room was lined with shelves, one of which held nearly a dozen oil lamps and a few gallons of kerosene, as well as several flashlights. Candles and batteries rested on another. Standing against the opposite wall was a small wood stove with an outside duct for venting. I was glad to see that if we lost electricity, we would still have both light and warmth. On the floor was a stack of blankets, along with a medical kit and a radio.

The rooms of the shelter were quiet. Strong brick walls and the earth around them muffled the sounds of war outside, but it was exactly those sounds that made the existence of this place necessary. The walls also helped block the bitter smell that had seeped into the rest of the house, although the soft, moldy scent of disuse filled the air.

Elsbeth prepared the bed in the small room for her mother. She unhinged the frame from the wall and brought it down to rest gently on the ground. She unfolded the sheets she had brought and tucked them in carefully around the mattress while I shook out the blankets.

At first Mutter refused to leave the kitchen, shaking her head when we tried to pull her out of her chair, and gripping the table so tightly that her knuckles turned white. We tried everything we could think of, until Elsbeth finally told her we needed help moving the ballroom picture of Hitler into the shelter. Reverently, Mutter pulled the huge picture down from the wall and carried it downstairs as if it were a baby. Elsbeth followed with the two red candles that always burned beneath it. Once in the shelter, Mutter placed the picture on the floor, gently propping it against a wall. Elsbeth carefully put one candle on each side. Then, going into the small room Elsbeth and I had prepared, Mutter promptly lay down on top of the bed and fell asleep.

✳

With each passing day the sounds of war crept closer. The thick walls of the basement could not completely block out the constant whine of planes overhead or the rapid sound of machine-gun fire that would begin loudly and then fade into silence.

During our second week in the shelter, we lost electricity and set up a system of oil lamps and candles to light each of the small rooms. Flashlights were to be used as little as possible to conserve batteries. There were only two small windows, both toward the top of the wall in the main room. They were lined with thick glass, like any cellar windows, and provided very little light.

Winter's cold soon crept into the basement, and

we kept the stove lit during the day as much as possible. I watched the stock of wood dwindle and wondered what we would burn once it was gone.

Elsbeth and I huddled together under a blanket during the day, playing cards or knitting. Mutter sat on the floor in front of the picture of Hitler, talking quietly to herself, almost as if she was praying that he would come and personally rescue us.

The few times we turned the radio on, we heard only static. There was nothing we could do but sit and wait for something to change, either for better or for worse.

Both Elsbeth and I were curious about what was happening outside. "Just a little peek? Can we just go upstairs for a little bit?" Elsbeth asked Mutter once when we had heard no sounds from outside for several hours. I stood next to Elsbeth, nodding, hoping for permission to go upstairs for just a minute or two.

"Nein!" Mutter replied sternly. "It is too dangerous. I won't allow it." Once we had convinced her to come into the shelter, it seemed she didn't want any of us to leave.

There were enough distractions during the day to keep my mind somewhat occupied. But at night I was still haunted by the images of the camp and questions about my family—my real family, which I had all but forgotten.

One night I awoke to gentle shaking.

"Eva. Eva, are you all right?" It was Elsbeth. Although I couldn't see her face in the dark, I could hear the concern in her voice. "Eva, you were crying in your sleep. What's wrong?"

"Nothing," I said. "Go back to sleep." How could I explain something to Elsbeth that I didn't even understand myself?

I knew she had noticed a change in me, however subtle it was. We still knitted together and played cards and talked for hours, but I could no longer be the German sister I had been, the one she had come to love.

✻

After three weeks in the shelter my body had adopted the routine of the sun, waking as it rose and going to bed shortly after it set. The windows offered some light during the daytime hours, but once darkness fell, it was difficult to do much of anything by the murky light of the candles.

Elsbeth had coaxed Mutter into eating regularly again, and the two of us were talking about venturing upstairs one day for our math lesson books. Boredom was fast becoming our worst enemy.

"It will only be a few minutes, Mutter," Elsbeth tried. "We'll hurry upstairs, get our lesson books, and be back. It's daylight. There haven't been any planes for hours. And we can bring you your needlepoint."

I could tell by the look in Mutter's eyes that Elsbeth had almost convinced her to let us go. Mutter was slowly returning to normal, and I knew that she, too, was bored. She had stopped crying for Peter, and the color had returned to her cheeks. Having her needlepoint would give her something to do.

"Well, I suppose—" she began, but was interrupted by a thunderous crash upstairs. There was another loud crash from outside the house, and then the ceiling above us was filled with the sound of heavy boots. There were shouts and barks in a language I had never heard.

"Russians. It's Russians. Oh, dear God." Mutter covered her shoulders with her shawl, and the three of us ran into her small room and huddled together on her bed.

The noises upstairs seemed to last forever. Doors opened and slammed shut. Loud thuds vibrated across the ceiling. Splintering noises cut through the air. Voices shouted back and forth. I was filled with helpless terror, knowing that we were trapped in our small basement shelter.

There was a crash at the entrance to the basement, and then three soldiers appeared in the doorway of our room. They were young but had full beards, and each carried a machine gun. They wore brown uniforms with matching hats and short black boots. Beside me Mutter gasped, and I took her hand. I had a sudden clear memory of the soldiers coming into my house, so long ago in Lidice. Tears sprang to my eyes. Was I going to be taken away again?

One of the soldiers had papers in his hand, and he waved them in Mutter's face. "Frau! Where are papers? Herr Werner? Where are papers?" he screamed in broken German.

Mutter shook her head. "I don't know. I don't—"

The soldier grabbed her roughly by the arm and pulled her off the bed.

"Mutter!" Elsbeth cried and stood, as if to go to her. But another soldier pushed Elsbeth back onto the bed and kept us both there by pointing his gun at us. Then the first soldier led Mutter out of the room and up the stairs. Elsbeth and I held on to each other and waited, trembling, for whatever was going to happen next.

The soldier nearest us smelled sour. I wasn't sure if it was the smell of fear or the smell of someone who had been fighting a long time. He had bright brown eyes that peered out from beneath his hat, eyes that never left us. Looking into those eyes made me wonder if the Russian soldiers were as cruel as the Nazis.

Finally, after what seemed like hours, Mutter came back with the first soldier. He threw her roughly onto the bed, where she lay, pale and shaking. Elsbeth grabbed her mother's hand while the soldiers talked quietly in Russian. They looked us over one more time, then left as abruptly as they had arrived.

From upstairs we could hear several rounds of rifle fire, accompanied by the sounds of things being ripped and broken. There was one final crash so ferocious that it rattled the bed we were sitting on. It was followed by a thousand tiny echoes of glass shattering. There came one last rumble of heavy boots on the ceiling, and finally silence.

Elsbeth went to her mother and gathered her in a hug.

"They are looking for Hans. They wanted all the papers from his office." Mutter spoke in shaky tones. "They took everything from his office. Everything. They tore up the house. They . . ." And she began to cry while Elsbeth rocked her gently, whispering soothing words to her.

✳

"We need a gun." Elsbeth declared before I was fully awake the next morning. We were lying in the bed we had been sharing in the large room. Through the tiny cellar window I could see that the sun was just beginning to rise. The fire in the stove had not been lit yet, so the air held a bitter chill.

"What?" I sat up, shivering and rubbing my eyes.

"A gun. We need to protect ourselves." Elsbeth's voice was determined. "I need to get the gun that's hidden at the target range in the woods. There could be more soldiers, and I will not be taken prisoner."

"Elsbeth! You can't go there. It's not safe. You can't." I thought of the hardness I had seen in the eyes of the Russian soldiers.

"Well, I'm going. You can come or stay."

"Elsbeth," I reasoned, "at least check your vater's office first. There are guns there, remember? I'll go with you to check upstairs."

We got out of bed and bundled into our coats. I looked in on Mutter, who was still sleeping soundly in the small room. Silently we crept up the stairs and peeked into the kitchen. The air was cold, and a delicate layer of frost covered everything in the room. All was quiet and peaceful, the sun almost fully risen. After being in the darkened basement for so long, my eyes took a while to adjust to the light. I stood, blinking and squinting, until I could fully open both eyes without pain.

I had forgotten how reassuring sunlight can feel. As we walked through the kitchen, it streamed through the two shattered windows and touched my face as if to say "Good morning." For a moment, I looked through the cracked panes into the backyard. Everything outside looked the same. A few patches of snow were on the ground, and the trees rose up proudly from the woods at the edge of the yard. The large gardening shed was still there, and the servants' house stood as it always had, almost as if it was mocking the war by remaining the same.

Inside, however, the house was a mess. Elsbeth and I walked through the kitchen and into the main entry hall, where Mutter's beautiful hand-sewn curtains hung in ragged shreds. In other places bits of broken china lay scattered on the floor. Pictures had been ripped off the walls, and the frames had been broken into several pieces. The photographs of Hitler were riddled with bullet holes. The dark wooden banister that ran along the spiral staircase to the second floor was splintered and jagged.

The huge final crash we had heard had been the antique crystal chandelier in the formal dining room. It lay on the floor, a thousand tiny pieces of shattered glass surrounding it as if they had each tried to flee the center of a blast. In the library a kitchen knife stuck out from a small photograph of Hitler, directly between his eyes. Dozens of books had been pulled off the shelves, their pages ripped out and shredded. Their remains littered the floor, looking like dirty clumps of snow.

The door to Herr Werner's office stood at a strange angle. Elsbeth nudged it gently, and it fell off in her hands. She leaned it against the wall, and we stepped inside to find the room empty of nearly everything but furniture.

"It's all gone," Elsbeth said with a frightened look on her face. "Everything," she repeated in disbelief, walking over to an empty gun case in the corner and opening its unlocked door. Her eyes glistened with tears.

"Elsbeth," I said, touching her arm.

She wiped at her eyes with her coat sleeve. Then, straightening, she looked at me and said, "We have to get the gun hidden in the woods, Eva."

"Oh, Elsbeth, it's too dangerous," I argued, thinking of the sounds of the planes and guns coming from outside.

"We'll go this afternoon, when Mutter takes her

nap." Elsbeth was determined. "It will be quick, Eva. We'll just get the gun and come back. We can't be left unprotected." Then softly she added, "Please?"

"All right," I said, and she took my hand and squeezed it.

Once Mutter was asleep that afternoon, we slipped on our coats. Elsbeth started up the stairs, but I held back, realizing that we would be going to a place near the camp. Instinctively, I felt for Grandmother's star pin. It was fastened, as always, to the inside of my skirt.

"Come on, Eva," Elsbeth said, stopping to look back. "Hurry."

I turned and followed her upstairs and out into the backyard.

Once again, my eyes shut momentarily from the brightness of the sun. The air held both the bite of winter and the promise of spring, and it felt glorious to be outside again. I stopped and took a deep breath, letting the fresh air fill my lungs. As my eyes adjusted, I opened them more and looked around, feeling a strange kind of freedom in being in a space so much larger than the confines of our small shelter.

I took another deep breath and noticed that the smell was still present. Again I thought of the camp and the women there.

Elsbeth trudged ahead confidently, seemingly unaware of the snow, the freedom, or the smell. She was focused only on finding the clearing and retrieving the gun.

At first I didn't even recognize the clearing. Only one tree still stood, its red bull's-eye glaring at us from the trunk. The other two trees lay in large jagged pieces, victims of either heavy snow or artillery fire. It was nearly impossible to tell where the boulder with the gun hidden under it was.

Frantically, Elsbeth began searching, randomly moving from one spot to the next. "It was here someplace. Perhaps over here," she said, trying to reach under the tangle of fallen trunks and branches. "Eva, help me!" she pleaded.

As I stood looking around the clearing, I realized the search was hopeless. "Elsbeth," I said gently, "the gun is someplace under the branches, and they're too heavy to lift. We can't get to it."

"No!" she said, throwing her whole body against a fallen branch.

"Elsbeth," I repeated.

She sank to her knees, her thick woolen stockings quickly becoming damp from the soft, thawing ground. Tears welled in her eyes. "You're right," she said quietly, shivering.

"Elsbeth. It's cold. You're wet. You're shivering. Start walking back and I'll look a little longer." I suddenly wanted Elsbeth gone. Now that we were so close to the camp, I was longing to go there, and I knew Elsbeth would never allow it if she was with me.

"No, Eva. I'll stay. I'm not that cold, and we need to find the gun."

"Elsbeth, Mutter may be awake. At least one of us should start back. I'll keep looking."

Elsbeth looked at me carefully. "All right. I suppose one of us should be there for Mutter."

I nodded, shooing her away with my hand. "Go. I'll be right behind you."

I watched her leave; then I turned and started walking quickly toward where I had once heard the Czech song, in the direction of the camp.

There had been no sounds of planes or gunfire so far, and this bolstered my confidence. I needed to see the camp again. Perhaps this time I could slip in through the barbed wire. Carefully, I picked my way through the snow and underbrush.

The loud snap of a twig made me stop. I froze. But then from behind a tree stepped Elsbeth, her face hard and cold.

"Elsbeth," I said, relieved. "You startled me. I—"

"I decided to come back. I was worried that you might get scared. But I can see you're not. And I know where you're going," she said, her voice flat, her words accusing. "I told you not to go to that place ever again." She was suddenly inches from my face. "I told you it's a bad place, filled with bad people."

"Elsbeth . . ." I wanted to explain. I wanted her to understand why I had to go.

"Are you Jewish?" Her question hit me like an invisible fist.

"What?" I could barely speak. "No. I'm not Jewish. What are you talking about?"

"I mean *were* you Jewish? Before you came here? I've heard of that, you know. Of Jews pretending to be true Germans. Is that what's wrong with you?" She spit the words at me like stones, sharp and painful.

Hatred burned in my stomach, its warmth spreading into my arms and legs. She was a Nazi. How could I have forgotten? She was a German who worshiped Hitler and hated all others. She was just like the soldiers who had taken me from my family. Just like Fräulein Krüger, who had sent Heidi and Elsa away. Just like Herr Werner, who was keeping my own people prisoner.

My mouth filled with a bitter, acrid taste. Without thinking, I punched Elsbeth hard in the stomach, then began hitting her over and over again with both fists. At first she tried to return my blows. But if there was one thing I had learned from having an older brother, it was how to fight.

Wanting to hurt her, I knocked her to the ground. I hit and pulled and scratched every part of her that I could, unleashing all my anger and frustration. She scrambled to get away, but I grabbed her foot, and suddenly we were both tumbling down a small embankment. When we reached the bottom, we finally lay separated, panting and staring up at the sky. Elsbeth was crying.

"Eva. I . . ." she began. Her voice was small and scared, and I was struck by how young she seemed at that moment. Her face was pale, and her eyes looked confused and frightened. She was older than I, but she was a child who knew nothing of the world.

I rolled over and stood up. Walking up the embankment, I grabbed my mittens and put them on. I was wet and cold, and I knew I would have bruises the next day, but at that moment I felt nothing, inside or out. The planes had returned overhead, and I knew it was foolish to try to go to the camp. Instead, I walked back toward the house, ignoring the quiet sobs coming from Elsbeth.

✳

I didn't speak to Elsbeth the rest of that day, trying as best I could to avoid her in the small space of the shelter. I was filled with anger, sadness, and confusion about what had happened in the woods, and I wasn't sure what to do with any of these feelings.

Elsbeth, too, stayed away from me as best she could. A sadness that I had never seen before rested in her eyes. Mutter watched us both with concern but said nothing. She was aware that something was wrong but could have no idea what it might be.

It wasn't until that night that I discovered Grandmother's pin was gone. Frantically, I searched everywhere: my pockets, my scarf, my skirt. But it was gone, lost back in the woods where Elsbeth and I had fought. The pin was the only thing I had from home, and I would not leave it, alone and cold, in the woods.

I waited in the darkness until the sounds of Mutter's and Elsbeth's breathing told me they were asleep. Quietly I reached for a flashlight and crept upstairs. I had no fear this time of what might be in the woods. I only wanted the pin back.

As I crossed the kitchen, I heard a creak and turned to see Elsbeth's face appear at the top of the basement staircase.

"Eva?" she called.

I didn't answer.

"Eva. Where are you going? Can I come? Please?"

"I lost something. I need to go back to the woods." My voice was rough.

"I'll help you look, Eva. Please?" She sounded lost and afraid, and I felt myself softening a little.

"Oh, I don't care," I answered, still feeling angry and confused. "Just hurry."

She went downstairs and came back a few minutes later, dressed and with a small flashlight in one hand.

Silently I led us through the woods, holding the light as low as possible to the ground. It was a cloudless night, and the moon provided some additional light along the way.

Near the target range I found the place where Elsbeth and I had fought. I could still see our footprints in the mud. I shone the light around the ground, looking for a glint from the pin. But there was nothing. An enormous sense of loss filled me. Elsbeth swept the ground with her light as well, unaware of what we were looking for but clearly trying to be helpful.

Even at night, the awful smell of this place filled my nose, and it seemed almost as if it was taunting me about the lost pin. I dropped the flashlight, sank to my knees, and let the tears fall. Elsbeth came to kneel next to me.

"Oh, Eva . . ." she said, putting an arm around my shoulder.

I let Elsbeth hold me and felt my anger at her ease as she rocked me back and forth like a child. I laid my head on her shoulder—the same shoulder I had hit and pushed earlier that day. She was the only family I had left.

When I stopped crying, Elsbeth helped me to my feet. I reached for the flashlight and followed the beam of light. It was pointed at an angle, to the side of the small embankment, and shining on something glittery. My heart raced as I ran over and picked it up. It was Grandmother's pin. The clasp was bent slightly, but all the garnets were still in place. I sighed with relief and clutched it tightly.

"Is that what you were looking for, Eva?" Elsbeth came to my side. "I have not seen it before. Where did you get it?"

I held it up to the moonlight so she could see. "It's my grandmother's pin. It is very special to me. I keep it with me always. I lost it when . . ." I couldn't say any more. I was still angry, but there was warmth and affection there, too. How could I love Elsbeth when she was a Nazi? And yet she was my adopted sister, and I did love her.

Elsbeth bit her lip and looked down at the ground. "Eva, I'm sorry. I didn't mean . . . I mean, I know you're not Jewish and . . . I don't know. I don't know anything."

"You're right. You don't know anything about me." I sat down, spreading my coat around me like a blanket. "I have my own mother and father, you know." I had been wanting to say these words out loud for so long. Just saying them made Mama and Papa seem closer and more real. "We live with my grandmother and my baby sister and my big brother."

Elsbeth sat next to me, shivering slightly but saying nothing.

"Someday," I continued, gathering courage to say what I really wanted to say. "Someday I'm going back to them."

"Eva," she said softly, "that's not possible."

"Yes, Elsbeth, it is. Someday I will go back to them."

"But Eva." She shivered again and wrapped her arms around herself. "I don't understand."

"No, Elsbeth, you don't."

We sat for a little while, and I scanned the sky for the North Star. Even if Elsbeth didn't understand, I did. I knew who I was, where I had come from, and where I would go someday.

"Elsbeth," I said, breaking the silence and pointing to the sky. "Do you see the star in the north, the one that's so bright?"

She followed where I was pointing. "Oh, the North Star. Yes."

"My grandmother told me once that if you are lost, you can use it to find your way home."

"How can you do that?" Elsbeth asked.

We sat for a while in the darkness while I told Elsbeth about the North Star, just as my grandmother had told me. Flashes of bombs had begun to appear once more in the distance, bright and sudden, and artillery fire had begun to sound. Now that I had the pin, I was again becoming aware of the reality of being outside during a war. It was dangerous. We needed to leave.

I stood and held out a hand to help Elsbeth up, then walked with her in silence back to the house and into the shelter.

✳

A week later I awoke with a start, sensing that something was wrong. I could see the outline of Elsbeth next to me, lying under the blankets in the same position as the night before. There was no noise in the basement. Nothing looked different in the murky darkness.

Quietly I walked upstairs, to find sunlight just beginning to make its way through the cracked windows in the kitchen, throwing spiderweb-like shapes of light across the walls. I squinted to help my eyes adjust.

Outside, the trees were signaling the beginning of spring. Their branches were covered with buds and filled with birds, singing and chattering merrily. I stopped, trying to remember the last time I had heard birds. Then I closed my eyes and listened carefully.

"Mutter!" I yelled downstairs. "Elsbeth! Wake up!" I raced down the stairs.

They both met me at the bottom, their eyes sleepy and fearful. "Eva, what is it?" Mutter gasped.

"It's quiet, Mutter!" I grabbed her hand and led her upstairs, with Elsbeth close behind. "Listen! Listen!" The three of us stood in the kitchen as several seconds passed in silence.

"It's quiet," Elsbeth whispered. "I don't hear guns."

"Or planes," I added, grabbing her in a hug. Mutter turned and led us back downstairs to the radio that had sat silent for so long. With trembling hands she turned the knobs until we could hear pieces of a broadcast, faint and full of static.

Germany had surrendered, the voices announced. Hitler was dead. Mutter looked at us, tears running down her face.

"It is over," she said quietly.

thirteen

June 1945: Fürstenberg, Germany

Iт felt strange to move out of the shelter and back upstairs. After so much time in the basement, my body had grown used to the darkness, and the brightness of daylight made my eyes ache.

Once we were settled in our rooms again, we spent days cleaning the rest of the house. Many windows had shattered from the constant rattle of planes, and we patched them with pieces of wood from the work shed. Some had jagged holes in them from gunfire. We patched those with smaller pieces of wood, trying to keep enough of the glass visible so we could still see through them. The result looked like a strange patchwork quilt.

It took hours to sweep up the tiny pieces from the broken chandelier that littered the floor of the formal dining room. Throughout the house a fine layer of dust covered everything, and we spent more days wiping tables, furniture, and woodwork, using torn bed sheets as rags.

There was no word about Herr Werner or Peter, despite Mutter's appeals to the temporary government that had been set up in Berlin. Mutter refused to go near Herr Werner's office or allow Elsbeth and me to clean or straighten it. Finally, after growing tired of walking past the empty reminder of her father, Elsbeth propped the door across the open frame.

"He'll put his office in order when he comes back," Mutter assured us. "Peter will help him. You know we aren't allowed in there."

"It's all right, Mutter. We'll just leave it for now." Elsbeth patted her mother on the shoulder, leading her back into the kitchen.

There was still no real food to speak of, although there was an adequate supply of canned goods left in the shelter. Relief camps were open in Fürstenberg, but Mutter refused to visit them. They were for the "poor" and the "needy," she said. According to her, we were neither.

It felt strange to be back upstairs in my pink bedroom. So much had changed both inside me and outside the house since I had last been in my room. I felt detached from it, the house, Mutter, and Elsbeth. My own kind of murky darkness had come to cloud my heart.

I had not been taken away from Elsbeth and Mutter, as I had feared. They were still my family. But ever since the discovery of the camp, I knew I could never fully be the German child I had once been. And the end of the war had not brought a rescue from Mama and Papa.

I felt as if I belonged nowhere and to no one.

❋

One morning, shortly after we'd finally finished cleaning the house and reassembling what was left, Elsbeth and I were in her room. We had slowly settled into a routine and Mutter had insisted we return to our lessons. She herself had begun to return to activities she had once enjoyed and she was downstairs with her needlepoint, while we were supposed to be working in our lesson books. But neither of us was really concentrating. Elsbeth was sitting on her bed, drawing little pictures in her book. I sat near her, propped up on one elbow and preoccupied with my thoughts. Suddenly, there was a loud knock at the front door, sharp and persistent. Elsbeth and I looked at each other.

"Who do you think . . . ?" Elsbeth began, but was interrupted by Mutter's screams.

"Nein! Nein!" Mutter's voice sounded anguished.

"Peter!" Elsbeth said, looking at me fearfully. "Something's happened to Peter."

Both of us raced down the spiral staircase to the front entryway. The door was open, and Mutter was huddled on the floor near a man and a woman who were standing in the doorway.

"You knew this day would come, Frau." The

man's voice was harsh and loud, his face unsympathetic and angry.

"Nein! Nein! It is not true. Lies, lies, all of it!" She reached out and grabbed his leg. "Please." The man roughly pulled his leg out of her grasp.

"Mutter!" Elsbeth knelt and put an arm around her. "What is happening?" she asked. "Who's lying?" She looked from Mutter to the man and woman. "Has something happened to Peter?"

I stood and stared, unable to move, somehow knowing why they were there. Both wore plain clothes with white armbands that had large red crosses on them. I saw no Nazi uniforms or badges, and neither appeared to be carrying a gun or club.

The woman was tall and slender, with short brown hair that framed her head in shining layers. Her eyes were dark, almost black. The man had red hair and freckles sprinkled across his pale face and arms.

"Are you Milada?" The woman stepped toward me and touched my arm. Her voice was quiet and soft.

Milada, Milada, Milada. The name shimmered in front of me, so real I could almost touch it. *Milada,* girl from Czechoslovakia, fastest runner in her school. *Milada,* best friend of Terezie, sister of Jaro and Anechka. Milada, who lived with her mama and papa and beloved grandmother.

I nodded and began to tremble fiercely.

"Milada," she continued, "we have found your

mother. She is alive. She is waiting for you in Prague."

I began to cry, brushing the tears away so I could see clearly and make sure this was not a dream.

"Nein!" Mutter stood, pounding her fists against the man's chest and shoulders. "Nein! Her name is Eva. She belongs to me. This child was given to me by the Führer. *I* am her mother!" The man put up a hand so her fists couldn't reach him.

I looked at Mutter, feeling oddly detached and barely even hearing what she was saying. Elsbeth took a step back, her face white and her eyes large and frightened.

"Eva!" Mutter cried, turning toward me. There was such pain in her voice, I had to look away. Swinging back to the man, Mutter cried, "You are disobeying the Führer's orders. You cannot take her!" Then with a sob she added, "You will break my heart."

"Milada," the woman said, "will you come with us?"

I looked at Mutter and then at Elsbeth, afraid at that moment that my own heart might break.

"My name is Milada," I said to the woman, needing to say my real name out loud. It sounded right and pure, and it filled me with joy. How long I had waited to reclaim my name! Then I added, "I want to go home."

The woman took my hand, leading me out the open door and into the sunshine.

"Wait," I said, stopping on the steps. "I have to get my things. I have to say good-bye."

"No, Milada," the woman said. "We will get you whatever you need. You need nothing from these people."

I felt for Grandmother's star pin, firmly fastened to the inside of my skirt, and I nodded.

Through the open door I could hear the sounds of Mutter weeping and Elsbeth comforting her. I tried to concentrate only on putting one foot in front of the other as I walked out to the white car that was parked in the driveway, *Milada, Milada, Milada* running through my head.

The woman who had come to the Werner house was an International Red Cross worker named Marcie, who was responsible for taking me back to Mama. She was from America but spoke both French and German. She was to be my escort on the long train ride from Berlin to Prague.

For many hours I sat on the train without speaking. A numbness filled me, the same sort of numbness I had felt after first leaving the camp in Poland to live with the Werners. I had been gone for three years. Three years. So much had happened in that time. Was it really true? Could I finally be going home?

Marcie was in the seat next to me, rocking slightly from the motion of the train. We both sat in silence, watching the scenery pass outside the window.

She told me that Mama had been staying in a center for displaced persons in Prague since being liberated from a Ravensbrück subcamp. I gasped when I heard the name Ravensbrück. Mama had been in a subcamp not far from the one Herr Werner had commanded.

I had never been that far from Mama after all.

The towns and countryside of Germany were nothing more than skeletal remains. Broken buildings littered the cities. Cows lay dead in the fields. Allied soldiers patrolled the roads. The people we saw walked with their heads bent low as they carried supplies or picked up debris.

Occasionally Elsbeth's and Mutter's faces would drift into my thoughts, and I forced myself to push them away. It hurt too much to think of either of them.

We entered Czechoslovakia late in the afternoon. Because the president had surrendered to Hitler without a fight, most of my country had been spared the devastation of war. It looked as I remembered it, proud and regal. Beautiful old buildings remained untouched and stood gleaming tall in the sun. The roads and fields looked peaceful and welcoming as we passed by. It seemed almost as if there had never been a war at all.

"It's beautiful, your country." Marcie sat next to me, following my gaze out the window.

I nodded. "America, I understand, is also very nice."

"Yes. It has its good parts. I enjoy seeing other countries, though."

I nodded again. "How much longer will the ride be?"

Marcie looked at her watch. "Another few hours. Your mother is very anxious to see you. You're all she's spoken of since she was freed."

"I can't wait to see Mama and Papa," I said. My voice caught just saying the words.

"Milada, there is something I must tell you." She touched my shoulder, and I could tell by her face that I was about to hear something unpleasant.

I grabbed the armrest of my seat, prepared to find out that I wasn't really going home. Perhaps this was just another lie and I was to be adopted into another family or returned to the center. I had been told so many lies over the past three years. How could I believe this wasn't another?

"Milada, I wish this wasn't what I had to say. But your papa and Jaroslav are not with your Mama. I'm sorry, honey." She stopped, clasping her hands together. Her voice grew softer. "Both of them were killed."

"No!" I cried, jumping to my feet, pain sweeping over me. "No! I don't believe you!" I screamed.

Marcie stayed calm. "It is true, Milada. I am so sorry."

I felt dizzy. "But the night they took us away, the Nazis told us Papa and Jaro had been sent to a work camp! They said . . ." And then I stopped, and my stomach lurched with the realization. Another Nazi lie.

Marcie gently pulled me back into my seat. Quietly, she continued. "The night you were taken, the Nazis led the men and boys to the Horak farm in Lidice." Her gaze remained steady. "There they were shot."

I felt myself go cold. "Grandmother?" I whispered, afraid I already knew the answer.

Marcie pursed her lips into a thin line and shook her head sadly. "She died in the Ravensbrück subcamp. But we are still trying to find Anechka," she added quickly. "She was adopted by a German family. We haven't been able to locate the family, but we *will* find her, Milada."

I stared at her, unable to speak, then turned back to the window.

"Milada," Marcie said, touching my arm.

I ignored her, continuing to focus on the trees that were moving past us.

"Milada?" she tried again, and I felt a tear roll down my face, followed by another and another, until I was crying so hard, I could no longer see out the window.

Marcie pulled me close, not speaking, and let me cry as we both swayed with the motion of the train.

✶

When we arrived at the displaced persons center in Prague that evening, it was spitting rain, staining the light brick of the building with dark blotches. Before the war the center had been a school. As I looked up at its entrance, I thought how strange it was that Mama and I were being reunited in the same type of building as that in which we had been torn apart.

Inside, I ran my finger along the polished lockers that lined the hall. Signs in German, Czech, and English offered directions to washrooms, doctors, and general assistance. Marcie led me down a hallway and around a corner before stopping at a small room where I had been told Mama was waiting.

"Your mama knows German, so you won't need me to translate," Marcie said.

"Yes. Good," I said. I was glad I would be alone with Mama.

"Are you ready, then?" Marcie asked, her hand on the door to the room.

I nodded, scarcely able to breathe.

"She has been in a concentration camp," Marcie said.

"Yes, yes." I couldn't hide my impatience. How much longer would I have to wait?

"You must understand her condition," she continued. "They were treated worse than animals in those camps. She will be okay in time, but right now she looks . . ." Her words trailed off.

"I understand," I said impatiently. I didn't care how she looked. I just wanted to see her.

"I'll be close by if you need me." Marcie opened the door, then disappeared around the corner. Mama and I were alone.

She sat in a chair, her hands clasped in her lap. Had I not known it was Mama, I might never have recognized the haggard, thin person who stared back at me. She looked like the women I had seen at the camp in the woods. Her hair was very short and ragged, with small tufts sticking out in places. Her knees were the widest part of her legs, protruding beneath her dress. Her cheeks were sunken and gray. But her eyes still shone with the light I knew as my mother's.

"Mama?" I reached a hand out to her. After three years, how could I dare hope that she was even real?

"Milada." She touched my face, pulling me to her and sobbing. I touched her with my fingers, needing to know that she was real, needing to feel every part of her: her hair, back, neck, hands, arms, shoulders. Over and over again she said my name. "Milada, Milada. My little Milada."

Long afterward, I would ask her to say my name just so I could hear it spoken out loud.

fourteen

October 1945: Prague, Czechoslovakia

W<small>HEN</small> Mama was well enough, she and I left the displaced persons center and moved into a small flat in Prague with Mama's cousin.

Our family of six had become a family of two.

Mama's cousin worked as an assistant in the office of the reinstated government. Like so many others, she was trying to help restore order after Hitler's troops had left. We could stay with her for as long as we needed her home.

I began part-time classwork at a school near the apartment, attending lessons in the morning and tutoring with Mama in the afternoon. All the lessons were in Czech, making them difficult and confusing. But I didn't care. I never wanted to speak German again.

Schoolwork kept me busy during the day, but my nights were filled with the faces of Jaro and Papa and

Babichka and Anechka. It was as if by dreaming about them enough, I hoped I might wake up one morning and see them standing in the small bedroom Mama and I shared. The few times I tried to talk to Mama about my dreams, she refused to listen.

"We must live in the here and now, Milada," she would say if I even brought up their names. Afterward she would go into our bedroom and shut the door, keeping it closed for hours.

Eventually I stopped speaking of them.

I kept Grandmother's pin next to me in a pocket of my skirt. I had shown it to Mama only days after being reunited with her.

"Milada," she had gasped, her eyes filling with tears. "You kept this? All this time? All these years?"

"Grandmother told me not to forget," I said, beginning to cry myself. "The night we were taken away. Remember?"

Mama nodded, grasping the pin. It was the only thing we had left from before the war.

The Czech language was coming back to me in bits and pieces. Sometimes I would remember a word or a whole phrase clearly, only to have it float out of my head hours later, just out of reach. Mama was trying to help, repeating words I pronounced incorrectly or reminding me of words I had forgotten altogether.

"Babichka," she said late one afternoon, when I had forgotten again how to say "grandmother" in Czech.

"Babichka," I repeated and looked down, suddenly swallowed by grief.

"Milada," Mama said gently, lifting my face to hers.

"I think about her all the time, Mama. And Papa and Jaro. And baby Anechka. I know you want us to live in the here and now, but I can't stop the dreams and I don't understand. I just don't understand any of it."

She wrapped an arm around me and pulled me down onto the small sofa next to her. "I don't understand either, Milada," she said, stroking my hair. "And maybe it's all right to talk. Maybe I'm ready for that now. A little."

I started talking slowly at first, then faster and faster, until the words came pouring out of me in a torrent. I talked about Elsbeth and her mother and about the center and Ruzha and little Heidi. About my discovery of the camp and the day Marcie came for me.

Mama talked too, but mostly about times long before the war. She told me about the day I was born and the day I was baptized. About her wedding day, when it had rained and rained and she and Papa had danced and laughed despite the mud. She told me about the last time she saw Babichka, who was led away because she was too old to work, and about Terezie, who was killed in Poland.

When Mama's cousin came home from work that night, she fixed us a small meal. Then she went into her bedroom and left us alone.

Mama and I talked late into the night, laughing occasionally and crying too. When we finally went to our room, I fell into bed, exhausted, and slept without dreams for the first time in months.

✻

Later that fall Mama and I went to visit the place where Lidice had once stood. Hitler's troops had razed the entire town, turning houses and buildings that had once been filled with our friends and neighbors into an empty field. The field lay before us, quiet and peaceful, a betrayal of the horror that had taken place there only three years before.

Mama and I stood together on top of a hill overlooking where the town had been. We were standing at almost the exact spot where Papa and I used to go stargazing. I took Mama's hand in mine. She looked at me and touched Babichka's pin on my collar. She had asked me to take it from my pocket and wear it so everyone could see it. It helped her to remember the good parts before the war, she said, and not just the bad things that had happened during the war.

It was late in the afternoon, and the sun was just beginning to set, turning the edges of the field a soft, hazy shade of orange. Squinting, I could almost see the place where our house had once been. In the breeze I could almost hear the voices of Papa and Jaroslav and little Anechka. And I thought I could even hear the voice of Babichka telling me to remember. Remember who you are. Always.

"They did not win, you know," Mama said quietly, looking out again over the field. "This war. Or taking you. Or Anechka . . ."

"I know." I looked out over the field, trying to imagine what Anechka would look like as a little girl. "They will find Anechka, Mama. They will."

She looked up at me and then out again across the field. One lonely star had appeared in the sky. I looked at it a long time before turning away.

I found my way home, Babichka, I thought. *And I'll remember. Always.*

Author's Note

Although Milada, Ruzha, and the other characters in these pages are fictional, this story was inspired by actual events that took place during World War ll.

By 1939, Hitler controlled the country of Czechoslovakia (now two separate countries, the Czech Republic and Slovakia). He assigned one of his favorite officers, Reinhard Heydrich, to be the "protector" of Czechoslovakia. Heydrich was known as a particularly brutal Nazi and helped develop the "Final Solution"—the plan to exterminate all European Jews. He was nicknamed the "butcher of Prague" by the Czech people and was greatly feared and despised.

After several years of planning in England, a number of resistance fighters parachuted into Czechoslovakia to assassinate Heydrich. Their attempt, made on May 27, 1942, did not go as planned, but Heydrich did eventually die on June 4 of wounds he received during the attack.

Hitler was enraged. Not only had the Czech resistance fighters killed one of his favorite officers, but they had shown a defiance toward him that he would not tolerate. He immediately sought revenge.

After a brief investigation, Nazi intelligence believed they had found a tie between the Czech resistance fighters and the small town of Lidice, located approximately fifteen kilometers (ten miles) from

Prague. It was later discovered that no one in Lidice had helped the assassins, but by that time it was too late. Hitler had taken his revenge.

In the very early hours of June 10, 1942, Nazi soldiers arrived in Lidice. They went from house to house, ordering residents to pack their things and leave for a three-day interrogation. The women and children were separated from the men and led to the Lidice grammar school. Their possessions were confiscated, and they were then taken to the high school in the nearby town of Kladno. As they made this journey, the Nazis assured them that they would soon be reunited with their husbands, fathers, brothers, and sons.

However, as the women were on their way to Kladno, the Lidice men and teenage boys were taken to the small Horak farm on the outskirts of town. In groups of ten they were lined up against mattresses propped along a wall to prevent bullets from ricocheting. Then they were shot. That night, 173 innocent men and teenage boys were killed, then haphazardly buried in a mass grave nearby.

Meanwhile, the women and children spent three agonizing days in the Kladno school gym waiting for word of their husbands, fathers, brothers, and sons. During this time the children were inspected by Nazi doctors. Their heads were measured and their eye and hair colors were examined to see if they matched Aryan standards. Although Milada was taken away from her mother and grandmother for the examination in this story, children often were accompanied by their mothers, and the records of some of those exams were recovered after the war. Those children who were deemed "suitable" were placed in the Lebensborn (which means "wellspring of life") program, a Nazi program that included kidnapping non-Jewish, non-German children who had Aryan features and "repatriating" them as German children.

Eventually, ten Lidice children over the age of one were selected for "Germanization." The youngest went directly to orphanages for adoption by German citizens. Others went through training in Lebensborn centers, where they were given German names, were taught the German language, and received lessons according to the Nazi philosophy. Unlike tens of thousands of other children who were put through the Lebensborn program, all the Lidice children still alive at the end of the war were found and returned.

In all, seventeen of the 105 Lidice children survived the war.

Very little has been written in English about the Lebensborn centers that housed kidnapped children, part of which may be due to the fact that so few children were found after the war. So the time Milada spends in the Lebensborn center is the most fictionalized part of this book. Her experience in the center has been pieced together from interviews and articles with and about the very few Lebensborn survivors, as well as research about the education of children during the Nazi regime and the overall Nazi philosophy regarding children and race.

A few things about the Lebensborn program are known for sure. Children (particularly Polish children) were literally kidnapped off the streets by Nazis known as "brown shirts" and placed in "retraining" centers. Some children—those like Heidi in the story who were unable to function in the horrific circumstances of the Lebensborn centers—were removed and sent to concentration camps, where their fate was almost certain death. Many of the youngest Lebensborn children who were recovered after the war were unable to remember anything of their former lives and were very traumatized when removed from their adoptive German parents.

The women of Lidice were sent to the Ravensbrück concentration camp near Fürstenberg, Germany, sixty miles north of Berlin. At Ravensbrück, the Lidice prisoners wore uniforms with a red upside-down triangular patch sewn on the chest. Inside the triangle was a black *T*, which stood for *Tschechisch*, the German word for Czech. This identified them as political prisoners, as opposed to the Jewish prisoners, who were religious prisoners and had a yellow star of David sewn on their uniforms. While many prisoners died of illness at Ravensbrück, others were killed because the Nazis considered them too weak or injured to work in the camp. Their bodies were cremated at the nearby Fürstenberg crematorium until 1943, when a crematorium was built on-site at Ravensbrück, followed shortly thereafter by a gas chamber.

Eighty-eight children from Lidice who were not seen as "suitable" for the Lebensborn program were taken to Poland. There they spent several weeks in a center with hardly any food and no extra clothing. After an additional six children were selected for the Lebensborn program, the Nazis took the remaining eighty-two children to specially designed vans near Chelmno, Poland, where they were killed with poisonous gas. Of the 500 citizens of Lidice, 340 men, women, and children were killed.

To complete his mission of revenge, Hitler ordered the destruction of Lidice. Nazi troops and prisoners from the nearby Terezin ghetto (Theresienstadt) spent a year erasing any evidence that a town had once existed there. All written trace of Lidice was removed from Czech records.

Although a new town of Lidice was eventually built, the old town was left as an empty expanse in order to serve as a reminder of the emptiness of war. Today, overlooking the site of the old town, are a museum, a sacred space, and a beautiful rose garden, all meant to help us remember what happened to this small village.

✳

In October 2004 I had the amazing opportunity to visit the Lidice Memorial in the Czech Republic and meet four survivors of the events of June 10, 1942. In addition, I met a man who was born shortly after the war whose mother had survived a stay in the Ravensbrück concentration camp.

Miloslava Suchánek-Kalibová was nineteen and her sister, Jaroslava Suchánek-Sklenička, was fifteen when the Nazis came to their village that night. Both spent three years in the Ravensbrück concentration camp and came back after the war to live in the new Lidice.

Václav Zelenka was four years old at the time of the tragedy. He was taken from his mother in the Kladno gym and put into a particularly brutal Lebensborn camp. He lives in the new Lidice and serves as the current mayor.

Maruška (Marie) Doležalová-Supíková was ten years old when the Nazis came on the night of June 10, 1942. Although I had already written most of the story before I met Marie, I discovered that her experience had an uncanny resemblance to Milada's.

Like Milada, Maruška lost her brother and father to Nazi guns, and lost her beloved grandmother in Ravensbrück. She too was adopted into a Nazi family and, like Milada, was able to keep a special piece of jewelry with her (a pair of earrings) throughout the war. Her adoptive family, like Milada's, lived relatively near Ravensbrück (although her adoptive father was not a high-ranking Nazi). Like Milada, she was unable to remember any of the Czech language when she returned. However, her mother did not speak German, and the two were unable to communicate. Tragically, her mother died several months after her return as a result of tuberculosis contracted in Ravensbrück. Maruška was left orphaned and alone.

I remain amazed not only by the courage these survivors showed sixty years ago but by their continuing optimism and strength. The story of Lidice has much to teach us about humankind's incredible capacity for brutality, as well as its incredible ability to survive—and even thrive—despite horrific events.

For more information, you can visit:

www.lidice-memorial.cz.

Click on the British flag icon for the English version of this website.